) go fishing. The next thing he knows, he is the unwilling owner of two stray kittens — and his mother is allergic to cat fur.

It isn't that David really wants to keep the kittens, but since he has them he feels a moral obligation to find them a suitable home. As a stop-gap measure he boards them with his fair-weather friend Snooper McGee, but the cats return home. The arrival of David's aunt and her dog only complicates the situation.

Like Penrod and Homer Price, David Keegan is often the victim of circumstance, attracting trouble like a magnet, but managing, ingenious American Boy that he is, to use his wits to turn his hilarious misadventures into success.

Two for Trouble

EILEEN ROSENBAUM

Two for Trouble

Illustrated by
JUDITH GWYN BROWN

Doubleday & Comp... ...c., Garden City, New York

Library of Congress Catalog Card Number AC 67-10056
Copyright © 1967 by Eileen Rosenbaum
All Rights Reserved
Printed in the United States of America
First Edition

To Alan with love

Chapter 1

THE TROUBLE WITH DAVID

David stood at the edge of the pond and stared down. Was this the right place? The water lapped gently at his feet, presenting a lopsided reflection of his face and the stick he held in his hand. He walked farther along the bank, gazing down. Everywhere the water looked the same. How could he tell where to start fishing?

With no one in sight to advise him, he selected a spot near a shady willow, flopped down, leaned back against the tree and picked up his stick. Fumbling in his pocket, he pulled out a length of string and a safety pin, attached them to the stick and was poised to toss the string into the water when he remembered.

"Worms!" he groaned. "I forgot about worms!" Now what to do? He glanced around, then down at his bag of lunch. Why not? If the food was good enough for him, it should do for a fish. Opening the bag, he gazed directly at a hard-boiled egg. He wouldn't mind getting rid of that! Breaking off a piece, he pushed it onto the pin, then tossed the string into the pond. As it hit the water, the egg shivered, slipped off the pin and disappeared.

"No fish would be dumb enough to get hooked for a hard-boiled egg anyway!" David thought, and peered into his lunch bag for something else. The peach was no good, David was sure of that. He briefly considered the pickle, then unwrapped the sandwich and found the solution. Bologna! Ripping off a long, thin strip, he jammed it onto the pin. It was the right shape and looked as though it should wiggle convincingly. He tossed the string into the pond again and leaned back against the tree.

Now all he had to do was wait for a fish. He stared intently at the string, then, as time passed, he stared less and less intently. Fishing, he decided at last, isn't the most exciting sport in the world. If Barney were with him it might be fun, he thought, but his best friend had gone to visit his grandmother for the summer. There was no one else around except Snooper McGee and Snooper was a jerk. Having nothing to do, David had decided to try fishing. At least it got him away from the house and his sister Diana, who was, he thought, the scrawniest, dopiest five-year-old pest in the world.

Tired of watching the string, David turned on his side and watched a column of ants move through the tall grass. Then he lay very still as some bees poked at the clover near his feet. When they had flown away, there was nothing left to watch, so David sat up and ate his lunch, saving the pickle for last.

"Boy," he thought, as he took a big, crunching bite, "fishing can sure be a drag when you run out of things to watch." He decided that when his pickle was gone, he'd pack up and go home.

There was a sharp tug on his pole. Something on the other end! David shoved the pickle into his mouth and took a firm grip on the pole. There was another tug. Carefully, he reached out for the string, grasped it and pulled it slowly out of the water. He expected an old tire, a shoe, a weed, anything except what came flipping through the air at the end of the string. He had caught a fish and a big one, too!

"Fish," he gloated as it flapped onto the grass and thrashed about damply, "you sure must like bologna!" David stared at it, wondering what sort of fish it was. It was a beauty, he thought, long and sort of whitish with a large popping eye on each side of its head. "I gotta get you home!" He picked up the fish and carried it over to his bike, then laid it gently in the basket. Before many minutes in the strong sunlight, it had developed a distinctly unpleasant odor. But that didn't matter. David whistled happily as he pushed his bike down the rutted track that lead from Piper's Pond to the highway, thinking how pleased his parents would be.

This would show them he wasn't sitting around wasting his time all summer. He could go fishing every day, save hundreds of dollars in grocery bills. Any fish that were left over he could sell. Who knows how much money he might make? It wasn't a bad plan for a boy who was eleven years old, going on twelve, and David knew his parents would love it.

If he could get into the house without being seen, he'd arrange the fish on the kitchen table with flowers around it for a centerpiece. Then his mother could cook it for supper.

He was halfway up the hill, pedaling hard, when he heard a strange mewing sound behind him. He turned and saw two large cats, one orange, the other gray, trotting behind the bike. Their tails stuck straight up in the air.

"Get lost!" David ordered, but the cats marched along without missing a step. A black and white tomcat leaped over a wall and fell in line behind the others. "You're wasting your time!" David snapped. "This fish is no cat-food!" But the cats tramped along, staring steadily at the fish in the basket.

Determined to ignore them, David pedaled steadily uphill. Behind him, a fat white cat and two scrawny kittens had joined the group. People on the street were staring, and it made David feel oddly itchy.

"Go climb some trees!" he muttered nastily. But his battalion of cats stayed in line and by the time he reached Highland Street, he counted six cats of varying weight and color following him. Two were puny little kittens who ran to keep up with the parade that turned up the driveway behind him. They stood at attention as

he parked his bike and lifted the fragrant fish out of the basket.

"Scram!" David shouted. "This is no cafeteria!" And he took the fish inside, slamming the door behind him. A note on the kitchen table read: "Diana and I at store. Back soon. Mom."

"That's a break!" David muttered. "When they get back, those moron cats'll be gone and I'll have the fish all fixed up." He laid the fish in the sink and ran cold water on it until the smell was less intense. Remembering where his mother kept her best silver serving platter, David got it and laid the fish carefully in the center. He was on his way out the door to pick some flowers for decoration when he discovered the cats on the back steps. Waiting. All six of them.

"Shoooooo!" he hissed, waving his arms wildly. "Scram! Get going!" The cats waited. David jumped and shouted at them, but not one moved. "Okay then, sit here for all I care!" He went back inside. Seconds later a cat's face appeared at the kitchen window. It was standing in Mrs. Keegan's flower box, beside a geranium.

"Get off there!" David shouted, but the cat stared through the window without moving.

"Those monsters mean business," David thought. "They'll park here forever unless they get a meal." He searched the pantry shelves and found two cans of tuna fish which he opened and shoved out the door. He heard squeals, scuffles, then silence. When he opened the door a crack and peered out, he saw two empty cans and six cats, sitting quietly waiting for the next meal.

"For cryin' out loud!" David shouted. "Go home!" These cats were going to spoil everything. His mother didn't like cats. In fact, she was allergic to them. They made her sneeze and get itchy all over. Whenever cats were around, Mrs. Keegan was a weepy mess.

David slammed the door shut and ran to the phone. He thought of calling the fire department, but decided that was only for cats in trees. He considered the dogcatcher, who also doubled as catcatcher. But the dogcatcher, like the truant officer, was a man of legendary evil who must be avoided at all costs. David stood near the phone, trying to remember which boy in his class had the biggest dog. Then he heard the back door slam.

"David!" Mrs. Keegan called, "what in the world are all those *cats* doing . . . ?" She stopped suddenly and David heard a noise that sounded like *glug*. "David," she called weakly, "what's this on my silver platter?"

"Boyo boyo boyo boy!" Diana cackled. "That's the biggest goldfish we ever had! How come it's not moving?"

David walked toward the kitchen, knowing that somehow his surprise had misfired. "Uh—hi, Mom!" he said casually. "How do you like it?" He took a deep breath and noticed that the fish had grown smelly again.

Mrs. Keegan, too, took a deep breath. "You caught *that* with a safety pin?"

David nodded. "And some bologna!"

"And you brought it home to surprise us?" Mrs. Keegan tried to smile.

David nodded again.

Diana stood over the fish staring at it. "Hi, fish!" she said solemnly, then reached up and poked it with her finger. "How come you don't move? What's the matter, you dead or something?"

"I caught it," David said, ignoring Diana, "and brought it home in my bike basket." He squirmed sheepishly. "I guess I collected a few cats on the way."

"Yes. A few," Mrs. Keegan agreed. "What shall we do about them?"

The door opened and Mr. Keegan came in. Before he could slam the door, two tiny kittens scooted in behind him. One was dirty white with an odd kinky tail. The other was dirty gray with ribs that stuck out like bony fingers. They squeezed between Mr. Keegan's legs, circled the room at top speed, then, suddenly timid, pushed between the stove and the refrigerator and stayed there.

"David, please!" Mrs. Keegan pleaded, her eyes already pink and moist. "Get those animals out of here! You know I'm allergic to cat fur!"

"What in the world are they doing here?" Mr. Keegan asked.

David explained hurriedly, trying to coax the kittens out of their tight little hideout.

"Try a broom!" Mrs. Keegan said, scratching her left

arm and wiping away a tear. "And if that doesn't work, call the dogcatcher."

Diana, who had been watching quietly, began to howl. And for once David didn't mind. "Not the dogcatcher! They're lost and the dogcatcher'll never find out who owns them!"

"All right, David, what do you suggest?" his mother asked, stifling a sneeze.

"Let us keep them for one night," David pleaded.

"One night! Just one night!" Diana echoed.

"I'll put them in the basement so they won't make you more allergic!" David promised. "Tomorrow I'll give them away. I know lots of kids that need cats."

"Odd," Mr. Keegan mused. "I hadn't heard about this sudden cat shortage." But he was smiling a teasing kind of smile.

"Please Mom, just for tonight!"

Mrs. Keegan shrugged her shoulders. "Keep them out of my way!" She sneezed twice, then left the room.

As though sensing their welcome, the kittens crept from their shelter. Diana immediately pounced on them. "I'm gonna call them Washing Machine and Dryer," she announced, getting a stranglehold on each kitten.

"What for?" David asked in astonishment.

"You don't need a what for!" Diana answered haughtily. "I just think they're two beautiful names." She turned to Mr. Keegan who had been admiring David's fish. "See what David brought home!" she exclaimed proudly. "Two cats and a goldfish!"

"That's some goldfish!" he replied, then turned to David. "You've got a real job on your hands, finding a home for these strays."

David knew he was right. It wouldn't be easy but it was a job worth doing. For the first time since Barney had gone away, David felt happy.

Chapter II

DAVID KEEGAN: DENTIST

David flopped onto his bed, hot and discouraged, his arms covered with dozens of tiny scratches. After having tramped around town all morning with a kitten under each arm, he was beginning to realize just how serious his problem was. Nobody wanted two mangy kittens. After ringing what seemed to be half the doorbells in town, he had brought them home, deposited them in the basement with a dish of milk and come up to his room to think. There must be someone who needed a pair of kittens!

An odd noise from Diana's room caught his attention. It sounded like crying, but it wasn't Diana's usual noisy howling. This was whimpering, soft and pitiful. David rolled off his bed, went out into the hall and opened his sister's door. Diana was sitting in a corner, weeping. When she saw David, she clapped both hands across her mouth.

"For crying out loud, what's the matter with you?" David demanded.

Diana shook her head, her hands still pasted firmly across her mouth.

"Are you going to answer me?" David demanded.

Again, Diana shook her head, tears flowing faster now.

"Okay, then I'm going," David said, turning to leave the room. A combination of curiosity and pity made him turn back. As he did, Diana lowered her hands to speak. "Stay here," she begged. When she opened her mouth, David saw the trouble. Right up front, there was a huge gap. Diana had lost a tooth.

"Is that all it is?" he asked, astounded at the fuss she was making. "A tooth?"

Diana's face was drenched in tears. "Yes," she sobbed.

"What's so bad about a tooth falling out?" David demanded. "It's great. It shows you're growing up. Besides, if you put it under your pillow tonight, the tooth fairy'll come and give you a quarter."

Diana shook her head. "Not growing up," she burbled. "Didn't fall out. I banged it out. That won't count for anything with the tooth fairy. Besides," her voice cracked tragically, "I wasn't supposed to."

"Supposed to do what?" David asked impatiently.

Diana gave a final heartbroken sob. "Walk with a box over my head. I promised mommy I wouldn't. But I did anyhow. I bumped into a tree and *this* fell out." She opened her clenched fist and there lay the tooth, completely wrapped around with Scotch tape.

David sat down. "You stuck a box on your head and

went for a walk. Right?" Diana nodded, wiping her smeary face on her arm. "You walked into a tree and your tooth fell out. Right?" Diana nodded again. "So what's the tooth all wrapped up in tape for?"

She hesitated. "I—I wanted to stick it back in."

David almost laughed. "Did it work?" he asked, swallowing his grin.

Diana shook her head. "Almost, David! I bet if you helped . . . !"

David interrupted her. "Don't be a dodo! Scotch tape won't put your tooth back!"

"How do you know?" she asked, again on the verge of hysterics.

"I just know," David said. "But if you really want me to prove it to you, come on, let's try. We'll go into the bathroom where there's a mirror."

Diana trotted after him obediently and in the bathroom he took the tooth from her, adjusted the crumpled tape, then made her lean over the sink, her face turned toward the light. "Hold still," he instructed and pressed the taped tooth into place. It didn't stick at all. "Aw, this is nutty!" David exclaimed. "You can't stick teeth back!"

"Try once more," Diana begged. "Please!"

"Okay, okay," David muttered. "But, like I said, it won't work."

Again Diana leaned over, her mouth open wide. David pressed the tooth in and let go. The tooth hung there, just for an instant, then dropped into the sink, rolled down the drain and was gone.

"Gone!" Diana wailed. "Now I got no tooth." And she clapped both hands over her mouth and began to whimper.

David, feeling responsible, tried to comfort her. "Look Diana, it doesn't matter. I'll explain to mom. Besides, the tooth fairy . . ." he paused, remembering there was no tooth for the fairy to claim.

Diana's face was wet all over and covered with dirty smudges. Her eyes and nose were an identical shade of red, and her hair stood out in dozens of little points and clumps. "I don't want mommy to know. I don't want daddy to know," she sobbed. "Now I got a big hole, looking funny and ugly. I don't want to be ugly. I want to be pretty." And she took a swipe at her streaming eyes with a grimy hand.

David spoke without thinking. "Don't worry, Diana!" he heard himself saying. "Mom and dad don't have to know. I'll get you a tooth and we'll put it in so there won't be a hole. I promise! Just stop that crying!"

In an instant, the cascade of tears stopped, a wide smile broke through and Diana said, "Okay, I stopped."

The promise was made and, impossible or not, David had to try to carry it out. Postponing the problem of the kittens for this more immediate one, he soon found himself downtown in front of a door with the words "Dr. G. BEAN, DENTIST" lettered on it. For perhaps the hundredth time, David wondered if Dr. Bean's first name might possibly be Green. Not being a particularly good friend of the Doctor, he had always been afraid to ask. Ever since the time he had bitten Dr. Bean's little finger, David felt that his welcome was less than warm. But Dr. Bean was the only dentist he knew. And so, he was here to ask for a tooth.

Acting bolder than he felt, he opened the door and walked into the waiting room. A small glass panel in the wall slid open and a mean-looking face appeared. It was a woman who looked as though she ate pickles for breakfast. "What do you want?" she asked, staring at the purple beanie David was wearing.

"I—I want to talk to Dr. Bean," David told her, almost in a whisper.

"Speak up, young man," she said sharply. "What do you want?"

"I want to talk to Dr. Bean," he repeated loudly.

"Dr. Bean's a busy man. Do you have a toothache?" She sounded as though she hoped so.

David shook his head. "I just want to talk to Dr. Bean." He couldn't think of anything else to say. But it seemed to work. After asking his name, she told him to wait and shut the glass panel.

David wandered over to a table which held several issues of a magazine called *Good Health*. He sat down in a chair and picked up the top copy. A boy and girl, all shined up and clean, grinned out at him from the middle of a field of flowers. Being so clean wasn't David's idea of a healthy way to live, so he dropped the magazine and began to dust his beanie.

The office door opened and Dr. Bean ushered a woman to the outer door. She looked as though she had a big wad of bubble gum in her cheek.

"Don't worry about a thing, Myrtle," Dr. Bean boomed. He smiled and his thick mustache spread like a bushy black bird that was about to fly away with his whole face. David was sure that Dr. Bean's mustache was meant to cover up his teeth which were crooked and not at all the pearly white choppers dentists were supposed to have.

The door closed and Dr. Bean turned to look at him, his mustache turning down into a hairy scowl. "Well, David, what can I do for you?"

"I was wondering if I—ah, could talk to you for a minute."

Dr. Bean shrugged. He wasn't anxious. "Come into my office."

Seated beside Dr. Bean's desk, David took a firm grip on his beanie and began. "I—ah—was wondering what you do with—well, what happens to the teeth you pull out?"

Dr. Bean frowned as though he didn't understand. So David repeated the question. "What I mean is, when you pull a tooth, what happens to it?"

Still frowning, Dr. Bean replied. "I throw it away."

"In the garbage?" David asked, having visions of searching Dr. Bean's garbage can in the dead of night.

"In the garbage," Dr. Bean agreed, happy that they had come to some small understanding. "Of course, there are a few—I mean if a tooth is interesting for any reason, I send it over to the University Dental School for the students to look at. But usually, I just throw it away."

David had his clue. "There are lots of things about teeth to study!"

Dr. Bean agreed.

"Do you think you might have a spare tooth around that I could study?" David asked hopefully.

"What in the world for?" Dr. Bean was distinctly startled.

"Well—uh—I've been thinking," David paused. Lies didn't come easily to him. "I've been thinking of becoming a dentist when I grow up and—I'd sort of like to study a tooth for a while and see if I like it."

"Odd ambition for a young boy," Dr. Bean mused, eyeing David suspiciously. "Still, I suppose there must be a few level-headed young men who realize at your age what a rewarding profession it can be." His mustache turned upward. "Of course I can find a tooth for you, my boy." He clapped him on the back, then paused thoughtfully. "You've changed a good deal since your last check-up. Your parents must be very proud." And with another clap on the back for David, he excused himself and left the room. Moments later he returned with a small container which he handed to David. "Here we are!" he announced, his mustache twitching with pleasure. "A splendid specimen. You take it home and study it. Get some books out of the library. You're well on your way to an honorable profession!" David shuddered slightly. "And if you need anything," Dr. Bean continued, "any questions you want to ask, don't hesitate to drop by." He gave David a final thump on the back and ushered him to the door.

"Fine boy. Quite a change," he mused. And David, container in hand, flew down the stairs, his heart considerably lighter.

Now he had the tooth. As soon as he figured out a way to stick it in, their problems would be over. As he pedaled up the hill toward home, David considered the possibilities. Scotch tape was out. So was any kind of glue. Bubble gum might work, or maybe peanut butter. As he turned the corner onto Highland Street, he was considering wire hooks. Maybe a paper clip twisted around the new tooth and hooked onto the teeth at each side would work. He'd have to hammer the hooks into place, but once that was done, the new tooth would be in to stay. But it seemed sort of complicated. David decided to forget about wire hooks.

He stowed his bike in the garage and hurried around to the back door, stopping to wave at his mother who was weeding flower beds in the back yard. He rushed through the kitchen, then stopped still. Caramels! The stickiest stuff in the world. What could be better? Just chomp—chomp and the tooth was in for life. He rummaged around until he found a bag of caramels left over from last Halloween, popped a handful into his pocket and rushed upstairs. Diana was waiting.

"Okay, let's go," he said briskly and led her into the bathroom, making sure to stay well away from the sink. "Here it is!" David announced holding out the container. "And here's what's going to keep it in." He showed her the handful of caramels. Diana grinned. Anything David said was fine with her. "Here," he instructed, "chew this caramel 'til it's good and gooey." Then he opened the box which held the tooth. There it lay, white and shiny, but strangely pointy-looking. It was all wrong! Diana needed a tooth for right up front. What Dr. Bean had given David was one of those fangs called eye teeth. Now what?

Unaware of the problem, Diana was munching away happily at the caramel, which was beginning to stick to the roof of her mouth. "It's gooey," she reported.

David shrugged. Maybe a pointy tooth in the front wouldn't look so bad. "Okay," he said, "shove the caramel into the place where your tooth was." Diana did as she was told. "Now hold still," he instructed. Picking up the tooth, he planted it firmly in the sticky caramel, adjusting it so that it hung straight down. "Smile!" he ordered, stepping back for a good view.

Diana grinned widely. The pointy tooth was bigger than her other teeth and hung down below them.

"Not bad!" David forced himself to say. "Not bad at all." He swallowed hard. "Of course, I don't know how long it'll stay in . . ."

"I want to see!" Diana demanded.

"Not yet," David said. "Wait for a while. Keep your mouth open so the caramel will harden. Best thing for it is air. Why don't you go outside and play so the tooth gets plenty of air?" He had to keep Diana away from a mirror, even if it meant playing with her all afternoon.

That night at the dinner table, David tried not to look at Diana. By ignoring her and keeping his parents attention away from her, he hoped to keep the fang secret, at least for a while. He had told her over and over not to use that tooth for chewing. In fact, they had even had chewing practice out in the back yard before dinner.

"I'm starved!" David announced, passing his platter to his mother and watching as she heaped it with buttered noodles, broccoli and two lamb chops. Lamb chops were bad news, he thought, as he remembered how Diana liked to gnaw them right down to the bone. With a lamb chop around, there wasn't much chance of the tooth staying in.

"How was your day?" Mr. Keegan asked pleasantly.

"So-so," David replied hurriedly. "I've been doing a lot of hunting around, trying to find out who owns those kittens."

Mrs. Keegan looked up. "David, do you mean to tell me we still have those animals in the house?"

David nodded. "In the basement. I can't give them away to just anybody, you know. First, I thought I'd try to find their regular homes. I figure there must be some kid just heartbroken about losing his pet." Mrs. Keegan began to scratch her arm, then the back of her neck. David continued quickly, "If that doesn't work pretty soon, I'll give them to anybody who wants them."

Mrs. Keegan scratched her shoulder. "Listen here, young man. Those kittens have got to go! On Thursday I'm having an afternoon tea for the Federated Charity Drive and next week your Aunt Melba is coming for a visit. She phoned me this afternoon."

"Aunt Melba!" David shouted. "That's terrific! When? How long?" Aunt Melba Cavendish, really the children's great-aunt, hadn't visited the Keegans since David was a baby. But she wrote often, and Diana and David loved her frequent surprise packages and letters. They especially liked to hear about Aunt Melba's dog, Fritz, who went wherever she did. Although Aunt Melba had never told them exactly what kind of dog Fritz was, David pictured him as a faithful collie or a German shepherd, a big sturdy pal of a dog. "How about Fritz?" David demanded excitedly. "Is he coming too?"

"Hold on there!" Mr. Keegan said with a smile. "Just give your mother a chance. She'll tell you all about it."

"She's coming next Saturday," Mrs. Keegan told them, "and she'll stay for about a week. She says she can't leave Fritz at home, though I'm sure I don't understand why. Anyway, she's bringing him along with her."

"Yippeeeeeee!" David shouted, completely forgetting his table manners.

"Yippeeeeeee!" Diana echoed, jumping up and waving her lamb chop in the air. Mr. and Mrs. Keegan turned to stare at her. Sunk deep in the lamb chop was a large pointed tooth and stuck to the top of the tooth was a large lump of caramel.

"What in the world . . . !" Mr. Keegan stared wide-eyed at the chop.

David sighed. "I knew it wouldn't stay in . . ." he began.

Chapter III

DAVID KEEGAN: ICEMAN

After several days of ringing almost every doorbell in Collington with Washing Machine and Dryer in his arms, David was ready to give up. It was only because he was so desperate that he went to Snooper McGee's house. Ordinarily, David stayed as far away from Snooper as possible.

"Hi, Mrs. McGee. Is Snooper home?"

"He's in the back yard, David," Mrs. McGee said with a sweet smile. "It's nice to see you. Why don't you come over more often?"

David's reply was polite but indistinct. Then he turned toward the back yard.

"Oh, David!" Mrs. McGee called after him. "When you go home, ask your mother if there's anything else she needs for her tea this afternoon other than the coffeepot. I'll send that over later."

"I will," David agreed and headed for the back yard. He found Snooper sunk deep in a hammock with only his nose visible over the top. That was typical of Snooper whose large nose led him everywhere, followed by huge sad eyes that didn't miss seeing anything. Snooper was a regular bloodhound.

"Hi Snoop," David said.

Snooper stirred lazily. "Where you been, anyhow?" he asked. "I been over your house a dozen times this week. Looked all over for you. Even went down to the playground in Mohasco Park. Thought maybe you joined the ball-playing guys." Snooper considered himself too intelligent to spend much time playing ball.

"Nope," David said.

"Then how come you disappeared?" Snooper asked accusingly.

"Just busy," David replied. "Look, Snoop, I came to ask you a favor."

Snooper sat up and studied David carefully. "What do you want?"

David took a deep breath. "Would you want to keep a couple of real swell animals for a while?" Snooper's mom was great about pets. In fact, she let Snooper do almost anything he wanted.

"What kind of animals? Rattlesnakes?" Snooper laughed a hoarse, wheezy cackle that sounded as though it belonged to a goat with a cold.

"Very funny!" David muttered, sorry he had started with Snooper. "They're cats. Just two nice little cats."

"Oh yeah. I heard about you trying to palm two mangy cats off on everybody." David wasn't surprised. Snooper hadn't earned his name for nothing. "If they're

so great, how come you don't keep them yourself?"
Snooper wanted to know.

"Because my mom is allergic to cat fur. It makes
her sneeze and cry and stuff. The only person who'll
take them is the dogcatcher and you know what he does
with little cats."

Snooper grinned fiendishly.

"Well, will you take them?" David hated to beg.

Snooper stared directly at him. "I'll take the old cats.
But not for keeps. I'll store 'em for you. And, it'll cost!"

"How much?" David asked, preparing to hear a wild
figure.

Snooper frowned, scratched his head and thought.
"Ten cents a day . . ."

"It's a deal," David cried.

"Not so fast!" Snooper said. "You didn't let me finish.
Ten cents a day for room. Ten cents a day for board.
Ten cents a day deposit. Not returnable."

"Is that all?" David asked glumly.

"Nope," Snooper grinned. "Ten cents a day for
taxes."

"Taxes!" David cried. "Whose taxes?"

"Mine," Snooper said. "You can't run a business
without paying taxes. My dad says so. That makes—
let's see—forty cents altogether. Forty cents a day and
I'll take the cats. That includes taxes. It's a real bargain.
Better think quick before my price goes up!"

David thought quick. The cats had to be out of the
house today. His mother, her eyes red and swollen, had
laid down the law. These kittens, though he didn't

really like them much, had become a personal crusade with him. They had a right to live just like everybody else. "All right," he said. "It's robbery, but I'll bring them over later."

"Payment in advance!" Snooper warned him.

David nodded grimly. In his bank there was enough money to pay Snooper for ten days. After that? Well, David didn't know what he'd do after that.

"One more thing," Snooper added casually. "I might borrow your bike a few times." Snooper had lost his bike and didn't have a new one.

"Wait a minute . . ." David protested.

"Just once in a while," Snooper said sweetly.

"Well, okay, but only when I'm not using it." And before Snooper attached any other conditions, David turned to leave.

"I heard your mom's havin' a swell party this afternoon!" Snooper shouted after him. "If the food's good, I'll be there."

If David could judge by the smells coming from their kitchen, the food would be terrific. The whole house smelled of cinnamon and butter and mint; and when David had left, his mother had been happily putting little colored cakes onto a silver tray. But as he returned, the scene was quite different. His mother and Diana, all tangled up with each other and a kitchen chair, were doing a strange dance all over the kitchen while Diana wiggled and cried. Fascinated, David watched them until he understood what was happening. Diana, wearing her white party dress with tiny furry lumps all over it, had untied her sash and twisted it round and round until she and the chair had become impossibly knotted together. Mrs. Keegan was muttering to herself grimly, while Diana howled something about horses and saddles.

"Can I help, Mom?" David asked, pitying her situation.

Mrs. Keegan surrendered Diana to the chair for a moment. "Yes, you can," she gasped, quite out of breath. "Ride down to Crocker Avenue and pick up a bag of ice cubes. It ought to fit into the basket of your bike. When you get home, put the ice in the refrigerator and change your clothes."

She gave him fifty cents to pay for the ice, then turned back to Diana whose squirming had left her more tangled than ever.

David pocketed the money and went outside. From the back porch, he saw Snooper preparing to ride away on his bike. "Hey, Snooper!" David shouted. "Leave my bike alone."

"I need it!" Snooper yelled over his shoulder as he pedaled away. David caught up with him at the corner where Snooper had stopped to let a car go by.

"You can't take the bike!" David cried, grabbing hold of the handlebars. "I was using it."

"You were not!" Snooper insisted.

"I was too!"

"Well, I need it," Snooper shouted. "My mom says I have to go over to the Finchs' and ask for our big coffeepot back so she can lend it to your mom."

"Then walk!" David snapped.

"Walk!" Snooper wailed. "The Finchs' live six blocks away. I'm not going to walk that far for any old coffee-pot."

"I need the bike!" David insisted, clinging to the handlebars.

Snooper sniffed angrily. "Look dope, if I don't take the bike, it's gonna take me all day to get over to the Finchs' and back. My mom's going to ask me why I took so long and then she's going to get mad. If she gets mad, she won't let me have the kittens. And if she doesn't let me have the kittens," he paused and, grinning horribly, ran his finger across his throat, "good-by kittens!" He leered at David. "So let go of the bike."

Defeated, David let go and watched Snooper ride down the street. He was in a jam again! If he explained to his mother why Snooper had a right to borrow his bike, he'd have to explain the kitten deal. And David was sure his mother wouldn't approve. She wanted those kittens gone for good! Boy, he thought angrily, a guy sure can get himself into a mess! Jamming his hands deep into his pockets, David felt the fifty cents for the ice cubes. Well, he'd have to walk to Crocker Avenue and carry the ice cubes home no matter how heavy they were.

Running downhill was easy. It was just a matter of keeping up with his legs which seemed to fly off ahead of him. In moments, he was around the bend on Crocker Avenue. Skidding to a stop in front of the ice machine, he pulled the fifty-cent piece from his pocket.

This was going to be fun. He'd never used an ice machine before.

The coin dropped into the slot; the machine whirred and rumbled, then was silent. David waited for the bag of ice to fall out somewhere, but nothing happened. He stared closely at the machine. A sign said "OPEN THIS DOOR." David was about to follow the instructions when he noticed something. There were two coin slots and two doors. One said "ice cubes." The other, where David had dropped his money, said "ice block." Biting his lip, David reached hesitantly toward the door, then threw it open. Inside, just as the sign said, was a huge block of ice, not wrapped or anything, just sitting there looking like an iceberg.

What a mess! How in the world was he going to get the thing home? Maybe it was lighter than it looked. David reached into the machine and gripped the block of ice, then lifted and staggered backward.

The ice was heavier than it looked, and impossible to see through, but David turned and took several uncertain steps toward the street. His hands were growing cold and numb and his arms began to throb with a frozen kind of pain. He wiggled a finger and found that he couldn't pry it loose from the ice. How would he explain frostbite in July? He bent and rested the ice against the side of the machine, then pulled his hands loose.

He had to get this thing home! If he didn't, there'd be a lot of explaining to do. And after Monday's tooth episode, things might be a bit rough for him. As he

gazed at the ice, he saw tiny beads of water begin to form on top of it. If he didn't do something soon, he'd have nothing but one large cold pool of water.

A dozen ideas came rushing through his head, all obviously impossible. Then, finally, came the idea that made some sense. In the vacant lot behind the ice machine, there had once been a pile of old boards, wheels, cans and other junk. Maybe, David thought desperately, something in the pile will help. He dashed around behind the machine. The pile was gone. The only things left were two rusty hubcaps and a greasy sack full of holes. These, David realized, are my only hope.

Snatching them up, he ran back to the ice, which was sweating freely now. He laid the hubcaps side by side on the ground and, with several grunts and a shiver, lifted the block of ice and placed it on top. Then he spread the gunny sack out on the ground, raised one edge and shoved the hubcaps and ice inside. Grasping the neck of the sack, he began to pull it along the ground. It worked! It was slow going and David had to walk backward, but it worked!

Getting the sack up and down the curbs was a problem, and the steep uphill climb made things even worse. But David made progress. With only two more blocks to go, he began congratulating himself. Then a car pulled to the curb beside him. It was Mrs. Ermish, the wife of Collington's Chief of Police. Beside her on the front seat was Mrs. Krantz, whose first name was Daisy but who reminded David of an eggplant.

Mrs. Ermish leaned out of the car window and

wagged a finger. "David Keegan, you should be ashamed! Out playing with some filthy bag when you're needed at home. Where is your sense of responsibility? Drop that thing and get into the car!"

"Thanks Mrs. Ermish, but I can't," David replied politely. "I've got to get it home."

Mrs. Ermish scowled at him. "Gracious, I don't know what's come over you youngsters. Chief Ermish says all young people are a little cuckoo these days." Mrs. Krantz nodded vigorously in agreement.

"Lack of discipline, that's what it is," Mrs. Krantz insisted. "Well, maybe your Aunt Melba can do something with you when she gets here. Always was a sensible girl, that Melba Cavendish. We were best friends when we were youngsters. Practically sisters." She smiled coyly at David. Her craggy face seemed to melt as she thought of time past. "A real sensible girl. Hope we'll get to see a lot of her."

"Of course you will!" Mrs. Ermish said forcibly. "They'll all be coming to the Police Department Picnic next Saturday. Melba will love it! Give her a chance to see old friends and all. Chief Ermish'll see that you get tickets." Then, remembering her annoyance that David wouldn't get into the car, she scowled darkly at him. "What in the world have you got in that disgusting bag? Whatever it is, it's leaking. You certainly can't expect me to put it in my car!"

David noticed a trickle of rusty-looking water seeping through the sack and winding back down the hill. "It's nothing much," he said. "I'll get it home by myself, thanks."

Mrs. Ermish shrugged her shoulders, rolled up the car window with a snap and drove away.

As he dragged the sack around the corner of Highland Street, David began to wonder about his Aunt Melba. What Mrs. Krantz had said worried him. Sensible usually meant trouble. The kind of kids grown-ups called sensible were the prissy, tattletale type. He hoped Aunt Melba wasn't like that. How could anybody who had a big terrific pal of a dog like Fritz be a crank? Impossible!

Within sight of the house, David began to plan the best way of sneaking in unnoticed. Most of the people were already there and he wasn't exactly dressed for a party. Greasy smudges covered his hands and his once-white shirt. He was sure there were plenty on his face, too. The gunny sack looked a lot worse than when he'd found it, kind of ragged and wet. A silent entrance seemed impossible for the hubcaps, which had shifted beneath the ice, clanked loudly with every step David took.

Many cars were parked near his house and the porch and lawn overflowed with people, mostly ladies in flowery hats, standing around in little bouquets. David stopped to consider the problem and lay out a plan of action. If he stayed in the street, keeping down low behind parked cars, he might make it to the driveway without being seen. The driveway, too, was lined with cars, and they would hide him from sight, so that he could slip around the garage and into the back door.

He came as close to the house as he dared, then eased the bag off the curb. Before ducking down behind the first car, David hurriedly surveyed the house. Diana was standing on the porch, eating her hair ribbon and staring directly at him.

"David!" she screeched "what do you have in the bag?" David groaned and crouched down behind a car but it was too late. Diana pushed through a knot of people on the porch and clattered down the stairs.

"David!" she hollered. "You got something for me?" She skipped down the street shouting his name. People turned to watch her. "Whatcha got in the bag?" she shouted, then stopped short. "It's bleeding," she screeched. "Something's in there bleeding. Hey, David, whatcha got in there that's bleeding? You got more fish, David? Is that what you have? You got a lion maybe? A dyin' lion?"

Several people snickered. David froze, hoping they'd turn away. At that moment, Mrs. Keegan came out onto the porch, a large tray of cookies in her hand.

"Mommy!" Diana waved her arms and shouted, the large gap in the front of her mouth plainly visible, "David's over here with a bleeding bag! He got something! Come and see!"

Mrs. Keegan walked slowly down the porch steps, staring strangely. "David," she called softly, "come here please."

David straightened up. With the sack clanking behind him, he moved slowly toward the house. It was very quiet and everyone was watching.

Chapter IV

DAVID KEEGAN: SHOWMAN

"Look, I don't care what I said. You have to take the kittens back!" Snooper insisted.

"Not so loud!" David warned, guiding Snooper away from the front door and over to the porch steps. "My mom thinks you took them for keeps."

"Well, I didn't and now you have to take them back!" Snooper said stubbornly. Whenever he frowned, his long nose stretched out even longer.

"But I want to know how come!" David demanded angrily.

"Because first of all, they're the nuttiest pair of kittens I ever saw. Washing Machine and Dryer!"

"Look, I told you to change their names if you wanted to. Those were just two crazy names Diana dreamed up. I don't even know which one is Washing Machine and which is Dryer!"

"Changing their names won't stop them from tearing our house apart, will it? My mom says they're scratching all the furniture and chewing up pillows and all kinds of stuff. Besides, they're always racing around like crazy and my dad keeps tripping over them. They're a lot of trouble!" Snooper sniffed haughtily, "And my mom says it's because they haven't had the proper training. Anyhow, she says I have to give them back." He hopped down the steps. "I'll bring them over tomorrow." He turned away.

David was furious. "You could at least stay and help me figure out what to do with them!"

Snooper shrugged. "Can't. On my way to the Gormans'. They're having a big party at their house, lots of aunts and cousins and stuff. Thought I'd go over and sort of hang around." Snooper knew about every party in the neighborhood. It was part of his snooping.

David watched him leave and flopped back against the top steps, careful to keep within the shade of the porch roof. Just inches away, the summer sun blazed down and it was a zillion degrees hotter. But the fact that he was cool didn't help David much. He was in a pickle. His mother would never allow the kittens back in the house, and David had given up the idea of finding someone to adopt them. Maybe the best thing to do was to turn them loose in the woods and hope they could get along by themselves. David knew it wasn't much of an idea, but it was the best one he had.

He looked up at the sound of footsteps to see Snooper hurrying toward him, his nose far in the lead. Snooper rushed up the walk toward David and planted himself on a step.

"I've been thinking about those poor kittens," he said, his voice brimming with sympathy. "We have to do something about them."

Snooper's change in attitude puzzled David. "Such as what?" he asked suspiciously. "What happened to the party at the Gormans'?"

"This is more important than any old party!" Snooper seemed annoyed at David's attitude. "We have to find a home for them! An idea is what we need and that's what I'm good at. Let's go over the whole thing and I'll give you an idea."

Though he was suspicious about Snooper's change of heart, David was glad to share the problem with someone. So, very carefully, he explained about the kittens following the fish to his house and his mother's allergies and his trips around town trying to give away the kittens.

"What did you do when you tried to give them away?" Snooper wanted to know.

"I'd go up to a house and knock on the door and ask if they needed a couple of kittens," David explained patiently.

"And what did the people do?" Snooper asked.

"Most of them were nice," David said, "but they'd tell me they already had a dog or a couple of cats or something. Anyhow they all said no."

"Then what?" Snooper asked.

"Then I'd go away!" David was growing impatient with all this pointless questioning.

Snooper stared intently at the porch floor. "The trouble is"—the words came slowly—"that people knew you were trying to get rid of them."

"What do you mean?" David didn't understand at all.

"I mean"—Snooper still appeared to be thinking hard—"that everybody knew these were just leftover kittens that nobody wanted. They were nothing special, just cats you had to get rid of."

"That's what they are!" David agreed.

"I know that!" Snooper said. "But if you want to get rid of them, you have to make them seem like something special. Something valuable. You have to give them as a prize or something. Maybe a door prize at a party or a show."

David was tired of Snooper's foolish ideas. "Terrific!" he snapped. "Except that I'm not giving a party or show."

"Why not?" Snooper asked triumphantly.

"What do you mean why not?" David was almost shouting now.

Snooper held up his hand for silence. "Why not have a show and give the kittens away as door prizes? Not returnable."

David stopped to think. It wasn't a bad idea. "But what kind of show?" he asked. "I can't give a show. The only thing I can do is play the bongo drums and that's not enough. I mean you have to have some good acts or puppets or acrobatics. . . ."

"Or magic!" Snooper said softly. "A supercolossal

magic show. Introducing Snooper the Great!" He leaped up with a flourish and took a deep bow. "I just got a Mr. Mystery Magic Kit. And it's great. You can be my helper. What do you say?"

David thought. "I say okay. It's a deal. Where and when?"

"Tomorrow in your basement," Snooper replied without a moment's hesitation.

David stared, realizing that Snooper didn't care one bit about the kittens. All he wanted to do was put on his magic act.

"Only this has to be a *big* show," Snooper continued intently. "Not just a few of the neighborhood babies, but lots of kids from all over town."

Well, David thought, I'll let him do his magic act. Just as long as I find homes for the kittens. "Okay," he agreed. "It'll be a big show. We'll have to advertise. Think up a supersensational announcement like they do when the circus comes to town. We'll print hundreds on the printing press I got for my birthday. Then we can plaster them all over town."

"Plaster them where?" Snooper asked.

"On billboards like the circus does," David replied.

Snooper sniffed scornfully. "That's not for free. Don't you know you have to pay to put those signs on billboards?"

"No kidding! Well, how about if we tape them to trees?"

"Against the law!" Snooper said shortly. "You can get put in jail for that!"

David scratched his head. Why did everything have to be so complicated? "There's got to be a way to advertise that doesn't cost money or get you put in jail."

Snooper was definite. "If I can't think of a way, then there isn't any."

David thought Snooper was acting pretty smart-alecky, but he couldn't think of a way either. "We're stumped!" he mumbled grumpily, slouching on the top step.

With a shriek, Diana dashed around the corner of the house chasing a balloon which bounced along just ahead of her. David and Snooper watched as it bumped up against a bush and slowly began to rise into the air.

Diana lunged at the balloon but missed. "David, help!" she shouted. "That's my best balloon. Get it back." The higher the balloon rose, the louder she shrieked.

"I can't get it. It's too high up," David said, as he watched the balloon float upward. "Get another one. There are lots more in the box Aunt Melba sent."

Diana stamped her foot. "I want that one!" she shouted. "It's the only purple in the box." The balloon drifted sideways at treetop level, then caught a breeze and began skipping crazily toward the roof next door.

"Look at it go!" Snooper marveled. "It's heading downtown. And I bet it gets there, too."

David's eyes opened wide and he felt as though his brain had opened, too. "Zowiee!" he shouted, jumping up. "I've got an idea!"

"What? What is it?" Snooper demanded. But the

screen door had already slammed behind David and Snooper had no choice but to follow him.

He found David at the kitchen table, pencil in hand, bent over a large sheet of paper. "Help me think of big, exciting words," David commanded.

"But where are we going to put the announcements?" Snooper demanded.

"Wait and see!" David replied and would say no more.

The boys worked for half an hour, mostly erasing and crossing out. At last the announcement was finished. It read:

ANNOUNCING
A SUPER SENSATIONAL
MAGIC SHOW
CHILLS! THRILLS! ALL STAR ACTS!
A REAL COLOSSAL SPECTACLE
Friday   2 o'clock
At 82 Highland Street
(In the basement)
Admission: 5 cents

Snooper sat back and admired their work. "Pretty good, huh?" he demanded, holding the paper up in the air.

"I'm not sure about some of the spelling," David said.

"Everything's spelled right. I'm sure," Snooper said firmly. "Come on, let's get these things printed. I want to see what your great idea is."

David smiled confidently. "Come on down to the basement. That's where my printing set is."

The Keegans had one of those dim, cool basements full of old things covered with sheets. There were terrific places to hide and, especially on a rainy day, it was a great place to play. The thing David liked best was the furnace and the coal bin next to it. His mother said they had the only coal furnace left in all of Collington, and David thought that was swell.

"I've never been down here before. Gosh, what a place!" said Snooper, whose own modern ranch house had neither a basement nor an attic.

"Neat, huh?" David agreed. "Bet you wish you had a coal furnace in your house," slapping its black iron side.

Snooper admitted it would be a fine thing to have.

"Bet you wish you could shovel coal in the winter like I do!" David showed Snooper the coal bin. For a moment, Snooper was respectfully silent. Then he turned away.

"How about this thing?" Snooper pointed to a wide tube that came down through the ceiling.

"That's a laundry chute," David explained proudly. "It runs all the way from the attic down to here. There's a little door in the wall on the first floor and the second floor and anything you drop inside falls down through the chute and comes out here." He pointed to a large basket underneath the open tube.

Snooper admired enviously. "Almost like a secret passage."

David agreed. "Sometimes in the winter, Barney and I use it to send messages in invisible ink. We even rigged up a pulley inside it that we can use to raise and lower stuff."

"That sounds like fun," Snooper said wistfully, then he moved away. "What's that big thing over there?"

David frowned ferociously. "A mangler!"

Snooper stepped back a few paces. "What does it do?" he asked quietly.

"It mangles!" David laughed fiendishly.

Snooper stepped back a few paces further. "Mangles what?"

Then David really laughed. "Sheets and pillow cases and stuff like that. It's sort of like an ironing board. Mom says that ages ago everybody had one. This one doesn't work, so it can't hurt you or anything, but you should hear the noise when it's plugged in. And what a name, huh?"

Advancing bravely to inspect the machine, Snooper paused and, arching his nose, gave a gigantic sneeze.

"Bless you," said David.

"I've never seen anything like this," Snooper said, referring to the machine.

David pulled out his printing set and laid it out on an old wobbly-legged table. He and Snooper began putting rubber letters in the slots and covering them with ink. After they had finished, David placed the paper, a piece at a time, on the inky type and pressed down. The announcements were smeary but readable.

"We have lots of great things down here," David

boasted as he slapped more paper onto the type. "We have an old radio from thirty years ago that sits right on the floor and is as big as I am. When you plug it in, a big old green scary eye lights up right smack in the middle."

"A green eye. Gosh, that's funny."

"What's so funny about it?" David was insulted.

"Not ha-ha funny. Strange funny. One time my dad was in Mexico visiting some famous old ruins and the guides told him about an ancient spirit called the Green Eye."

"I don't think it's the same green eye," said David, no longer insulted.

"I don't think so either," Snooper agreed and paused to sneeze again. "That Green Eye guarded a gold mine or diamond mine. I can't remember which. Anyhow, when the Spanish invaders came, they all broke into this mine. Then guess what happened?"

"What?" David was interested, even if it wasn't the same green eye.

"Killed," Snooper announced flatly. "Every one of them killed. The natives called it the Curse of the Green Eye and no one ever went near that mine again."

"Gosh," David marveled. "That's a great story." He grinned. "This green eye doesn't guard anything but an old coal bin."

"So what?" Snooper sneezed again. "Coal is almost like diamonds, isn't it? I learned that in geography. Or was it science? Come on. Let's explore your coal bin."

The announcements, twenty-five in all, were finished and spread out to dry.

"What about the show?" David asked, annoyed that Snooper's urge to snoop always got the best of him.

"Okay," Snooper agreed reluctantly and sneezed again.

"What's the matter, you allergic or something?" David asked. "You've been sneezing like crazy."

"I don't know. My throat feels kind of funny, too. I guess it's nothing. Let's get going with these announcements. I bet your idea's not so hot!"

"Wait and see!" David repeated as he gathered up the announcements and started up the stairs. Leaving Snooper at the head of the stairs with instructions to wait, David ran into the kitchen, stopped to talk to his mother, who was peeling potatoes for supper, then dashed out the back door. He was back in a moment with a bicycle pump, a ball of string and pair of scissors. Beckoning for Snooper to follow him, David carried his odd collection of items out to the front porch, sat Snooper down and curtly instructed him to cut the string into short lengths with the scissors. He disappeared for a moment and returned with a large box in his hand.

"Behold!" he announced dramatically and, dipping into the box, pulled out a handful of colored balloons. "Each balloon will be blown up and a string tied to it. And attached to each string will be an announcement for our show. We'll send them floating all over town."

Snooper was impressed. And jealous. That sort of idea should have been his instead of David's. But David had thought of it first. He shrugged away his annoyance and began cutting string.

When the balloons were finally blown up and the announcements attached, the boys divided them into two bunches and took them out to the middle of Highland Street. There they stood, the balloons forming a fat colored umbrella over their heads. "Ready. Set. Go!" David cried and as the boys released them, the balloons bounced and drifted away. Some were slower than others to catch the breeze and a few were snagged in tree limbs. But David and Snooper were confident that anyone in Collington who was interested in balloons would soon know about their show.

Now that they had carried out David's part of the plan, Snooper seemed to take charge. "Let's go," he said briskly. "We've got to practice the magic act. There isn't much time." And he sneezed a gigantic sneeze.

Chapter V

DAVID KEEGAN: STAR

A basket of plastic geraniums hung on the McGees' front door and as David stood facing it, waiting for Snooper to answer his knock, he whistled a tune that was wobbly but definitely cheerful.

Today was going to be a superterrific one. Not only would he and Snooper have a great time giving a show, but the kittens would be off his hands at last. Then tomorrow, Aunt Melba and Fritz would be here. A dog like Fritz was a pet worth having, David thought with a swell of pleasure, not a pesky nuisance like Washing Machine or Dryer.

David had no doubt that the kittens were as good as gone. After all, nobody turned down a *prize*, no matter what it was. David remembered when Mr. Candless, the school principal, had given the right answer to a telephone quiz question and won sixteen cases of Diaper-Dew, some stuff that was supposed to make babies' diapers smell great. Mr. Candless didn't have any babies, he didn't even have a wife; but he was still happy about the prize. The stuff was delivered to the school and sat in the corner of the gym, collecting dust, for almost a year until finally Mr. Withers, the janitor, gave it away to the Collington Hospital.

David knocked again, wondering what was taking Snooper so long. Finally, the geraniums swung away and there stood Mrs. McGee, a huge bottle of nose drops in her hands.

"Hi, Mrs. McGee. Can Snooper come out?"

Mrs. McGee shook her head. "Sorry, David. He's in bed with a terrible cold. It might be grippe or virus or even a case of flu." She paused thoughtfully. "Or maybe it's just a cold. Anyhow he needs plenty of rest, lots of fresh fruit juice and"—holding up the bottle—"nose drops!"

It took David several seconds to realize what this news would do to his plans. By that time Mrs. McGee had told him a polite good-by and closed the door.

David raced around to Snooper's room which faced the back yard. "Psssst, Snooper!" he hissed into the open window which was just above his head.

"What do you want?" asked a twangy, stuffed-up voice from inside the room.

"Hey, it's David. Come to the window!"

"I can't," the voice replied peevishly. "I'm sick."

"Well, what are we going to do about the show?" David wanted to know.

"I don't know. I don't feel so good. She keeps putting these blacks drops in my nose!"

"You have to help me think!" David pleaded.

"Who can think with a nose full of black drops?" Snooper asked pitifully.

"What are we going to do about the show?" David demanded.

"I don't know," Snooper replied listlessly. "I'll let you have my magic set if you want it."

"I can't do any of those tricks!" David said angrily. "I don't know how!" Realizing that was all the help he would get from Snooper, David turned away.

"My mom says I have to give the kittens back any-how!" Snooper called after him. "And you owe me a dollar sixty for room and board!"

David wheeled his bike down the McGees' driveway to the street, got on and pedaled slowly toward home. A horn honked behind him. Realizing he had been riding in the middle of the road, David quickly swerved to one side. The rubbish truck rumbled past and Mr. Pludder, David's best grown-up friend, waved cheer-fully at David. Further down the street the truck stopped for some rubbish. Mr. Pludder hopped off the little platform at the back of the truck and waited for David to catch up. Whenever he could, David rode the rubbish truck and helped Mr. Pludder. People threw away the greatest stuff and David was allowed to keep almost anything he wanted. So far he had saved a pith helmet, just like the African explorers wore, except that it had a small hole in it; half a dozen assorted-size wheels; and a big box full of some kind of tickets with numbers on them. There were lots of these numbered tickets in books and as soon as he could think of something to do with them, David planned to use them.

But today, David was in too much trouble to think about enjoying himself on the rubbish truck, so he waved half-heartedly at Mr. Pludder, who swung up onto his little platform and waved back as the truck clanked around the corner and out of sight.

As David turned into his own driveway, Diana rushed out the front door wearing a moth-eaten gray blanket and a pointed hat, carrying an old mop. "David!" she shouted. "I'm ready to be in your show! I got my witch costume on. I couldn't get a broom, so I'll be the kind of witch that rides a mop!" She cackled, showing the large gap where her tooth had been.

Mrs. Keegan followed Diana onto the porch, and David noticed that she was dressed for going out. "There isn't going to be any show," she told Diana gently, then she turned to David, who had parked the bike and was coming up the steps. "I just spoke to Mrs. McGee dear, and she told me about Snooper's cold. I'm sorry you have to cancel your show, but maybe you can plan it for another day." She opened her purse and took out the car keys. "Frankly, I'm just as glad," she confessed. "With your Aunt Melba coming tomorrow, I have a million little things to do. Now that your show is off, I can do some shopping. I'll only be gone for a few hours. You'll find your lunch on the kitchen table. Diana's already eaten." Mrs. Keegan bent to kiss David. "You won't mind keeping an eye on her, will you, dear?" David nodded numbly and Mrs. Keegan left.

David and Diana watched her drive away, then Diana turned to him accusingly. "How come no show?" she demanded. "I got all ready!"

"Aw, dry up!" David snapped. He was upset by the fact that his mother had taken the whole thing so lightly. Of course, she thought Snooper had taken the kittens for keeps and didn't know anything about the plan to give them away as door prizes.

"Well, you better have a show!" Diana insisted loudly. "That big, tough boy, Louie Krebs, came over before and he said to tell you he's coming and you better have lots of all-star acts and chills and thrills like the balloons said."

David stared at his sister. "Did he really say that?"

Diana nodded importantly. "Can I be in it? Can I be the witch?"

"I don't know," David said in a troubled voice. "I've got to think. I'm going in to eat my lunch. You stay around." The screen door slammed behind him, and he glanced up at the grandfather clock in the front hall. One o'clock. Just an hour before the show was to begin. He paced slowly down the hall. Two things stood out in his mind. He was scared stiff of Louie Krebs. And he had to get rid of those kittens. Therefore, he reasoned, there had to be a show. But what kind? He passed the basement door and remembered briefly how much fun he and Snooper had had down there yesterday. In mid-step, he stopped and froze as an idea flashed into his mind. In a moment, the plan seemed as simple and clear as though it had been arranged for weeks.

Turning, he dashed back to the front porch where Diana sat, sadly twirling the strings of her mop. "Okay, the show is on and you're in it!" he told her.

Diana hugged her mop in excitement. "I'm going to be the scariest witch in the whole wide world!" she gurgled.

"No, you're not going to be any witch," David insisted. "If you want to be in the show, you have to do just what I tell you." And he took away her mop, sat her down on the porch steps and told her just what to do. And for once, she did it.

By one-thirty, she was back from Snooper's house, staggering under the weight of a large cardboard box which held the two kittens covered over with Snooper's magician's cloak.

Meanwhile, David had been dashing around the house collecting pencil, paper, tape and scissors, his bongo drums, a floppy old rainhat and, most important, his Mitey-Brite flashlight with the red and green filters. With all this equipment in his arms, he rushed down the basement steps and within minutes, had placed everything just where it was needed. He was back upstairs in four hair-raising jumps to give Diana her final orders.

Because there was no one else to help, David had to allow Diana, whom he usually trusted with nothing at all, to collect the money and lead the audience downstairs to the basement. He wished desperately that

Snooper's nose drops would magically cure him, but knew that such a wish was hopeless. He crossed his fingers and told Diana what to do.

"Then tell them to line up in a long line," he finished, "and bring them down to the basement. It'll be dark, so go slow. Tell them to sit down on the floor. Then come into the laundry room. Got that?"

Diana nodded vigorously, her scraggly hair flapping across her face. David raced back downstairs. A few more minutes and he was ready. He snapped on Snooper's cloak, jammed the floppy rainhat down on his head. Then he pulled the shade on the one small window, snapped off the overhead light and looked around. It was as black as a tar road at midnight.

When he heard the hollow thud of many pairs of feet near the stairs, he groped his way into the laundry room and settled down near the door to wait for Diana. In a moment, he heard her shrill voice.

"Pssssst, David. Hey; it's scary in here. Where are you, anyhow?"

"Not so loud!" David hissed. "Over here. Where is everybody?"

"Sitting on the floor!" Diana answered. Incredibly, she had done exactly what David had asked her to do. "I don't like it down here!" she whispered. "It's too dark."

"That's part of the show, stupid," he answered, but he spoke kindly, for she had been a real help to him. "Now listen," he said, pushing the bongo drums into her arms. "I want you to start banging a slow scary beat on these drums and keep banging 'til I'm finished."

"I don't know how to play these!" Diana protested.

"Well, start learning!" David wrapped his cape about him, turned and tiptoed out the door. The bongos began an uneven wavering beat and, as David tiptoed toward the center of the basement, he heard a few whispers and a nervous laugh.

"Silence!" he commanded in his deepest voice. Placing the beam of the flashlight halfway under his chin, he switched it on. The red filter threw a weird shadowed light on his face. The old hat, pulled down low, deepened the shadows. "Welcome to the tomb of the Green Eye," David boomed.

"Aw, baloney!" jeered a voice that David recognized as Louie Krebs.

"Welcome to the cave of the Mangler!" David continued smoothly. "If you wish to speak, rise and approach the Mangler, slave of the Green Eye!" As he spoke, David aimed the flashlight's red beam at the old mangler and threw a switch. The mangler shivered, groaned, and occasionally clanked. The bongos beat unevenly in the background.

"Who wishes to speak to the Mangler? Step forward please," David commanded. There was a pause during which the mangler gave several loud groans.

"What—what does it do?" It was Louie Krebs speaking again, but this time his voice sounded thin, almost timid. David could tell by the sound that he hadn't moved one inch.

"It mangles," David boomed. "At the command of the Green Eye." He paused. "Silence!" he ordered. "The Green Eye will appear!" David switched off his flashlight, and the basement was totally black. No one stirred. He groped with his hand until he found another switch which he turned until he heard a click. Slowly, a pale green circle appeared, seemingly from nowhere. It grew brighter and brighter until finally it glowed a vivid throbbing green. There was a small light green dot in the center.

"The Green Eye will now speak," David announced and he turned another knob. There was an ear-splitting squawk, then a long crackle of static.

"The Green Eye has spoken. The Curse of the Diamonds is lifted!"

"What curse?" asked a timid voice.

"Silence!" David ordered. "And I will tell you the story of the Green Eye." He moved away from the Eye, switched on his flashlight and in a slow, mysterious voice, repeated the story Snooper had told him about the spirit of the diamond mine. In David's version, the location of the mine was changed from ancient Mexico to ancient Collington.

Near the climax, David paused and noticed that Diana was pounding away steadily on the bongos. Then he continued. "His greedy fingers touched a diamond. It was cold, deadly cold." David paused again. "Suddenly, the Green Eye spoke. And that was the end of the greedy man and all his friends. The Eye placed a curse on the diamond mine and for the next thousand years, no man entered it. Today, at last, the curse is lifted. The mine, home of great treasure, is open to anyone brave enough to enter." He shone his flashlight on the coal bin. "The Green Eye welcomes you to the diamond mine. Who will be the first to enter in search of fabulous treasure?"

There was a long, long silence. The bongos were quiet. Finally, a low voice said, "I will." David realized with a silent snicker that it wasn't tough Louie Krebs who had spoken, but little Harvey Marks.

"Wait!" David commanded. "I will show you the way." Switching off his light, he tiptoed to the laundry room door where he had laid three extra flashlights.

"Pssssst, David, I'm scared. It's too dark down here." Diana's voice quivered unhappily.

"Clam up, will you? You'll spoil everything!" David hissed. He tiptoed back to the basement where Harvey Marks was waiting. "Rise, brave warrior!" he commanded Harvey.

"Robert wants to go with me," Harvey said as he tugged Robert to stand up beside him.

"Uh—sure I do!" Robert agreed lamely.

"Follow me, brave warriors." David led the boys through the inky darkness toward the coal bin, then placed a flashlight in Harvey's hand. "Turn this on only after I close the door behind you," David said sternly. "When you want to come out, knock twice. And remember this," he added, raising his voice so that everyone could hear him clearly. "Some of the diamonds are disguised as lumps of coal. One of you, or maybe even two, may find a magic lump marked with a white X. Anyone finding a magic lump will receive a priceless treasure to keep forever." David stressed the word *forever*. "Each person may bring out only one lump," he warned. "Remember, the Green Eye is watching you!" and he closed the door behind them.

Everyone listened breathlessly, expecting to hear hair-raising screams through the door. But they heard nothing except the pebbly sound of coal being moved, then a giggle, and finally the cry, "Wow, here's one with a white X!"

David sighed happily. So far so good. Harvey Marks had earned himself a priceless treasure. To make the thing more convincing, David had decided to call the kittens The Royal Sons of the Green Eye. Luckily, both kittens did have green eyes but David wasn't sure if they were anybody's sons. For all he knew, they could be daughters.

"Hey!" Louie Krebs called to David. "How come you didn't let me in there first?"

"Cause you didn't ask," David replied calmly.

"Yes I did!" Louie whined. "Didn't I Willie?"

"Yeah," growled Willie Harris. "Maybe you didn't hear him, but he asked."

"Okay Louie, I hear you now," David replied. "You and Willie can both go. But remember, the Green Eye is watching you!" That seemed to calm them down some and as David handed him a flashlight, Louie's hand trembled.

Once the door had closed behind Willie and Louie, everyone else began clamoring to go inside, except Diana, who was at David's side complaining of being scared. In order to get rid of her, David sent her upstairs to get the kittens and bring them, in their box, to the top of the stairs. Then he lined up the rest of his audience, led them to the coal bin, gave away the last of the flashlights and watched as they filed inside. Then he sat down outside, sighed with relief and listened to the shuffling and laughing inside. Everyone seemed to be having a swell time in the coal bin and David could hear cries of "I think I found one!" "This is a diamond, for sure" and finally Louie Krebs' gravelly voice shouting, "Here's one of those white X things!"

David opened the door. "Time's up!" he called. "The Green Eye commands us to leave," and obediently the boys shuffled to the door and surrendered their flashlights. David led them through the basement, carefully avoiding the Eye, then up the stairs.

At the top landing he found Diana and the carton. Reaching in, he pulled out a scrambling kitten in each hand. He gave one to Harvey and the other to Louie, explaining that they were the absolute Sons of the Green Eye. Both boys were too astounded to do anything but clutch the squirming kittens.

As they came out into the light of the hallway, David noticed two things. The first was that each boy, except for the whites of his eyes, looked as though he had been dipped in black paint. The second was that

Mrs. Keegan was standing in the hall, staring wide-eyed at the strange parade.

"Gosh, Mrs. Keegan, that diamond mine's great!" Willie Harris said excitedly. "I think I got a real diamond here!" he exclaimed, holding out a lump of coal. "But Louie found one with a white X and he got one of those Royal Sons."

"Yeah," Louie agreed, hesitating a bit with confusion, "this is a Royal Green Eye—or something."

"Hey!" Robert shouted, "you guys sure look funny!" The boys stared at each other's blackened faces and hands and, laughing and talking excitedly, they trooped down the hall and out the door. David was left to face his mother. She rubbed her forehead, then scratched her arm.

"Don't tell me!" she sighed. "I don't want to hear a word! Royal Eyes! Diamond mines! I wouldn't understand it anyway. Just tell your father about it when he comes home. And explain it to those boys' mothers when they call." She turned away, shaking her head. "Diamond mine!" As she climbed the stairs, she seemed very tired.

David shuffled into the kitchen and sat down. In a few minutes, the phone began to ring. By nightfall, both of the Royal Sons of the Green Eye had been returned with regrets and David knew he had failed again.

Chapter VI

DAVID KEEGAN: DOG TRAINER

As the bus pulled into the Collington station, Mrs. Keegan was just completing a long lecture that had David squirming and Diana giggling because, for once, she had escaped without any of the blame.

"Now I mean it, David!" Mrs. Keegan said firmly. "If those animals are not out of the house *for good* by tomorrow morning, I personally will deliver them to the pound. This nonsense has gone on long enough. One day they're gone. The next day they're back. I've been as patient as I possibly can. Now I *must* draw the line. Tomorrow. And that's final! Is that clear?"

David nodded glumly. Tomorrow morning he'd take the kittens down to the woods near Mohasco Park and turn them loose. Terrible as that was, it wasn't as bad as turning them over to the dogcatcher. Even his excitement at meeting Aunt Melba and Fritz couldn't erase the misery he felt when he thought about the

kittens. He had failed. There was no getting away from
it.

The bus door swung open and, as passengers appeared,
David anxiously waited for Fritz to emerge. Several
gray-haired women could have been his Aunt Melba
but none of them had a dog. One by one, tired men
and women and cranky children came down the steps
until the last, a small, thin woman who appeared wide
awake and stood straight as a poker. Her gray hair was
done up in thick braids that were twined round and
round her head in a complicated pattern. On top of
the braids sat a hat that looked like a tiny bird's nest.
She wore a dress covered with pictures of vegetables
in various lifelike shades and over one arm, though the
weather was far from chilly, she carried a coat, an
umbrella and a sweater. In the other arm she held a
suitcase of a sort David had never seen before. Staring
directly at the Keegan family, she strode down the steps.
She and Mrs. Keegan hugged and kissed and David
turned away, embarrassed at all that mush and per-
plexed by the fact that Fritz was not to be seen.

As Mrs. Keegan left to collect the luggage, Aunt
Melba turned her attention to him. "So this is David!"
He turned back and allowed himself to receive a leathery
kiss and a long, silent head-to-toe inspection. Diana was
given the same treatment but immediately began chat-
tering about all the dolls she had at home who were,
at this very moment, waiting to celebrate Aunt Melba's
arrival with a super-duper tea party. And so it was quite

some time before it was quiet enough for David to ask about Fritz.

Aunt Melba smiled a tiny pinched smile and tapped the odd suitcase at her side. "In here, safe and sound!" she said. "Fritz is not too fond of traveling. It'll be a few days before he's himself again." David stared at the suitcase. It was much too small to hold a collie or German shepherd unless he was a tiny puppy. Too confused to ask any further questions, he followed along silently as his mother and Diana escorted Aunt Melba and her luggage to the car. Diana took advantage of his silence to begin a long story about their pets. "We have goldfish," she announced importantly, "and we had a turtle but he died. We had kittens too, but I guess we don't have those any more."

"Ugh!" Aunt Melba shivered. "I simply cannot abide cats. Nastiest, sneakiest animals in creation! Never understood how people could have them around. Despicable creatures!" She shivered again.

"You won't have to worry about these cats!" Mrs. Keegan said, with a long look at David.

During the ride home, Mrs. Keegan and Aunt Melba carried on that sort of pointless grown-up conversation about who had gotten married, who had had babies and who had moved away in the long time since Aunt Melba had been back home. David, ignoring most of the talk, kept his eyes on the strange suitcase beside Aunt Melba on the front seat. He offered to carry it from the car to the house, but instead Aunt Melba gave him her coat and umbrella. He and Diana followed her up the wide front steps onto the porch and stopped short as she paused and announced briskly that it was grand to be back. They trailed her into the house and stayed with her as she inspected the entire downstairs. Aunt Melba seemed to favor a lot of inspecting.

Finally, Diana could stand it no longer. "You really have a dog in that suitcase?" she demanded. Aunt Melba stared at her, eyebrows raised.

"It is not my habit to make jokes," she replied and prepared to open the suitcase. She swung back the lid and reached in, pulling out what looked to David like the handle of a basket with a big blue bow attached to it. It was a basket. In it lay a fluffy blue pillow and on the pillow sat the strangest little animal David had ever seen. It looked like a cocoa-brown feather duster with a cramped, cross little pop-eyed face in the middle.

"Say how-do-you-do, Fritz!" Aunt Melba crooned.

Fritz growled and showed tiny little pointed teeth.

Aunt Melba sighed. "I told you he wouldn't be himself. Then, of course, he's not too fond of children. But once he knows you, you'll be great friends!"

"But what is he?" David blurted out.

"Do you mean to say, young man, that you've never seen a Pekingese?" Aunt Melba was astonished.

David admitted he hadn't and hid his disappointment by pretending to examine the animal. But he stayed a safe distance, for Fritz's beady black eyes were staring suspiciously at him.

Diana ran to Mrs. Keegan and clutched at her leg. "I don't like him!" she declared.

Mrs. Keegan comforted her. "Are you sure, Aunt Melba—I mean he doesn't seem to care for the children. Maybe if we put him in the basement, just until he gets used to being here."

"I wouldn't dream of putting Fritz in the basement!" Aunt Melba said. "He's not that sort of animal, Janet. He's delicate and sensitive."

David didn't know anything about delicate and sensitive, but he did know that Washing Machine and Dryer were in the basement and wouldn't exactly welcome Fritz's company.

"Uh—how about if I take Fritz for a walk," he suggested.

Aunt Melba bent close to Fritz, who was sitting tensely at the edge of his blue pillow. "Fritz would enjoy a walk," she announced as though the message had come directly from Fritz himself. Without further delay, she reached into the suitcase, pulled out a red leash with small sparkling stones on it, and snapped it onto a collar that was buried somewhere in the fur of the animal's neck.

David took the leash gingerly and headed for the door. Fritz stalked crossly behind him. "You want to come too?" he asked Diana, thinking, in a very cowardly way, that he could turn the beast over to her and take off.

"Nope." Diana said, "My dolls need some more tea." Aunt Melba accompanied them to the front door and paused to inspect the sky. "I do think it might rain," she said.

"Maybe we better not go out!" David said quickly.

"Nonsense. Rain never hurt anybody if he's properly dressed for it." Dipping into the suitcase once more, she pulled out several unidentifiable items which she began to fit on Fritz's paws. It took David a full minute to realize they were tiny red rubber boots!

"There we are!" she said. "Now for the raincoat and hat!" And impossible as it seemed, Aunt Melba pulled out of the suitcase what proved to be a red plaid raincoat and matching beret, topped by a large pompon. David shuddered with embarrassment.

"Now young man," Aunt Melba instructed briskly, "Fritz will wait while you get a raincoat for yourself." Though David had had no intention of putting on a raincoat, he turned and obediently went to find one. Somehow, it was hard to disobey Aunt Melba.

Returning, David took the leash and led Fritz out onto the porch. The sky was gray, but not the sort of gray that meant rain. Fritz trotted sedately down the steps, made a smart right turn and headed up Highland Street, the pompon on his hat bobbing importantly. David had intended to walk on Summit Street where there were not many people who knew him, so he gave the leash a gentle tug. Fritz ignored the pull and continued to march along, his red rubber boots squeaking on the pavement. With each step, David became more concerned. If they continued in their present direction, they'd pass Snooper's house and once around the corner, they'd be on Park Street where the big kids hung out. David desperately did not want to be seen with this dressed-up dog, especially since, to admit the truth, Fritz seemed to be the boss.

David gave the leash another tug, harder this time. Fritz turned, gave him a swift view of little pointed teeth, and resumed his march toward Snooper's house. Having no other choice, David followed. He was so warm inside his useless raincoat that rivers of perspiration began to trickle down his back.

As they approached the McGees', David closed his eyes, held his breath and let the dog lead him. He opened them just once to glance hurriedly at the house. Snooper was not to be seen. Fritz continued his quick trot and after a few more paces, they seemed to be out of danger. The next house was the Gormans' and Mrs. Gorman was hardly ever at home.

But a pile of old cartons and boxes at the curb attracted Fritz's attention. Turning sharply to the right, he marched toward the pile and began snuffing and burrowing for treasure. They were in plain sight of Snooper's house.

"Come on, you mutt!" David growled and gave the leash another tug. Fritz responded with an angry snarl and continued rooting in the junk pile. Evidently, he smelled something that he meant to have and in the process he overturned a few boxes and pushed his beret to the side of his head.

Then two things came out: the sun and Snooper McGee. Snooper stared and cackled as he came down the street toward them. Meanwhile, the sun was beating down on David in his slicker.

Snooper leaned up against a tree and smirked. "Are you and your brother," he inclined his head toward Fritz, "expecting a storm?"

David would have punched him except that the leash was in his right hand, which was his punching hand. By the time he transferred it to the other, the urge had left him. "Look you. No smart remarks!" was the best reply he could think of.

Snooper studied the dog who was still busy in the junk pile. "Don't tell me *that* is the mighty Fritz!" David had done a good deal of boasting about the terrific collie his aunt was bringing to visit. "What do you call that, a shrunk up collie?" Snooper doubled up against a tree, honking with laughter.

"You have eyes, don't you?" David replied angrily. "It's a Pekingese. Everybody knows that!" David gave the leash a tiny tug. "Come on, Fritz, let's go."

"Aren't you going to let me pet him before you go?" Snooper asked, still smirking nastily. "I never petted a Pekingese with a raincoat on before." He advanced toward the dog, hand outstretched.

Fritz froze and gave a low, nasty growl. Snooper snatched his hand back and retreated quickly.

"Not very friendly, is he?" he muttered, the smirk fading.

"He knows who his friends are," David replied coldly, and since Fritz seemed to have abandoned the junk

pile, David tried a hopeful, "Let's go, Fritz!" and followed the dog toward home.

"Hey, well, I'd like to be his friend!" Snooper shouted after them, his composure recovered. "I'll be over around four."

"Don't bother!" David shouted back, but he knew that wouldn't stop Snooper. And he was right.

When Snooper arrived, just after four, David's mother, sister and aunt had gone to visit Mrs. Ermish and left David at home to dog-sit. According to the instructions Aunt Melba had left, it was time for Fritz to be brought downstairs. After having had his afternoon nap in the peace and quiet of Aunt Melba's room, Fritz, who was not used to stairs, had to be carried down in his basket. David had been elected to do the carrying.

"Where's the dog?" Snooper wanted to know.

"Upstairs!" David replied shortly. "I have to bring him down soon."

"What do you mean? He can't come down by himself?"

David shook his head and explained about the stairs. He was so disgusted with Fritz that he was ready to take even Snooper into his confidence. "You know, the mutt is so dopey, he doesn't even play with a ball or a rubber mouse or anything. He," David shook his head sadly, "plays with a doll!"

"And you have to carry him up and down the stairs!" For once, Snooper wasn't smirking. "It's unfair."

"Wait 'til you meet my Aunt Melba!" David declared.

"As long as she's here, she decides what's fair and what's unfair." He paused thoughtfully. "Maybe I should just say to her, 'Aunt Melba, I don't want to carry your dog up and down the stairs.' Maybe that'd work."

Snooper shook his head. "That never works with grownups. They don't care whether you want to do something or not!"

"Still," David said thoughtfully, "There ought to be another way."

"How?" Snooper's sniff dismissed the idea. "You haven't got an elevator."

David's glum face lit like a bulb. "Oh, yes we do!" he said. "Remember the laundry chute? We used it mostly for secret messages but I don't know why it wouldn't hold a dog's basket."

Snooper hadn't been listening. "Gee, Dave, that's okay! A great idea. You tie the dog onto the rope . . ."

"Not the dog! The dog's basket. With the dog in it. Then we lower away and the person on the first floor unties the basket."

"Great! Terrific! He'll love it! Let's go!"

David and Snooper ran upstairs to Aunt Melba's room, where Fritz was sitting at the edge of his blue pillow and, it seemed, waiting for someone to carry him downstairs.

"Hi, Fritz old boy!" David approached cautiously, motioning Snooper to stay back. "How about being the first passenger in the Keegan Express Elevator." David was convinced that Fritz, who was a very lazy dog, would love the trip. He lifted the basket and carried it into the hall, setting it down near the laundry chute. Then he opened the small door halfway up the wall. The inside looked like a wide chimney and there, just as David had said, was the rod. Draped across it lay a sturdy length of rope. David was really looking forward to this. It had been a long time since he'd used the laundry chute for anything except dirty shirts.

"Everything's here," he told Snooper. "You go down and open the little door in the hall outside the kitchen. I'll lower him and you can catch him. Whatever you do, be careful. We don't want him to get hurt."

As he listened to Snooper clop down the stairs, it occurred to David that this whole project was a bit cockeyed. He was sure Aunt Melba wouldn't be too hot on the idea. She was awfully particular about how Fritz was treated.

"Okay, I'm here. Lower away!" Snooper shouted up through the chute.

David thought. What harm could one ride do? Gently, he lifted the dog's basket and tied a secure knot around the handle. Fritz frowned at him.

"Don't worry, boy!" David said. "We'll be careful." And holding the basket in one hand and the loose end of the rope in the other hand, he swung the basket slowly into the laundry chute.

Then things began to happen! Fritz looked around, gave a soprano yelp and nipped at David who, as a matter of reflex, drew back his hand. The basket plunged into the chute and down.

"Catch it!" David shouted to Snooper, but Snooper

had time to do nothing but blink as the basket plunged past.

David was sure that the soft pile of laundry in the basement would cushion Fritz's fall. But that didn't mean the dog was safe. Fritz was about to meet Washing Machine and Dryer.

David flew down the stairs, grabbed Snooper's arm and pulled him along to the basement. The scene was awful. Fritz, yelping frantically, was in retreat; but the kittens, arched, hissing and spitting, had already done some damage. A fluffy tuft of fur was missing from Fritz's right ear and the blue pillow in the basket was shredded in three places.

Lifting Fritz beyond the kittens' aim, David remembered Aunt Melba's comments about cats. This certainly wasn't going to improve her opinion of them. Or of him, either. Having no other choice, he turned to Snooper.

"Snoop," he pleaded, "you have to do me a favor!"

"What do you want?" Snooper asked suspiciously.

"Take the kittens back," David begged.

"No, siree. Nothing doing. Not on your life!" Snooper's nose folded up like an accordion.

"Just 'til Saturday!" David pleaded. "I'll let you use my bike!"

"Don't need your bike!" Snooper answered. "I saved up enough to buy one of my own. It's kinda beat up but it's better than nothing."

"Sure!" David said angrily. "With all the money I paid you for keeping the kittens, you buy yourself a bike! Now I know why I got them back all of a sudden. You didn't need any more money!"

"Well, so what?" Snooper asked defiantly.

"So now, I really need help. Please take them back. Just for a couple of days!"

"What'd you ever do for me? When your pal Barney is around, I can go jump in the lake!" Snooper stared at David, then turned away. "Okay, give me the darn kittens! I'm going home. I sure don't want to be here when your aunt gets back!"

Chapter VII

DAVID KEEGAN: BUSINESSMAN

"Don't bolt your food, Harold!" Aunt Melba scolded as Mr. Keegan swallowed his toast and gulped the last of his coffee.

David was fascinated. He had never heard anyone speak to his father that way. What was even more amazing, Mr. Keegan did what he was told.

Aunt Melba glanced at the bowl of red, orange and yellow Sugar Snappers Mrs. Keegan had placed in front of Diana. "Janet, what sort of a breakfast is that for the child? Red cereal!"

Mrs. Keegan shrugged meekly. "It's what they like, Aunt Melba," and as though to prove it, Diana bent over her dish and began slurping it up.

"Diana! Such noises! And your nose is nearly in the plate. Sit up straight, my girl!" Aunt Melba turned back to Mrs. Keegan. "I do not approve of such dreadful food." She glared at the vivid cereal. "Nutrition is what's important. Vitamins, minerals, health-giving, vigorous growth foods. Nature's own nourishment is what growing children need!"

David was anxious to finish his breakfast and go someplace quiet where he could plan a way to dispose of the kittens. Snooper had agreed to keep them until Saturday, but that was the final deadline. Since Aunt Melba was watching, he ate his Sugar Snappers as slowly and neatly as he could. But David needn't have worried. Aunt Melba was ignoring him as though he weren't even there. Yesterday's incident with Fritz had convinced her that he was beyond all help.

Aunt Melba carefully folded her napkin and placed it next to her plate. "Janet, I think I should like to go downtown today. There are a few small items I'd like to purchase. Can you come along?"

Mrs. Keegan shook her head. "Afraid I can't, Aunt Melba. The repair man is coming to work on the washing machine this morning." Her face brightened. "Why not take David with you? I'm sure he'd love it."

Aunt Melba raised an eyebrow and slowly turned her head toward David as though she'd never seen him before. "Oh yes," she said. "David."

To his own amazement, David heard himself volunteering eagerly. He was anxious to get back into his aunt's good graces. The cat problem would have to wait.

"Very well," Aunt Melba agreed, but she wasn't exactly jumping for joy. Fritz was to stay at home. The trip would be too much for him.

As they started off down the hill, David noticed that his aunt didn't walk, she marched, her red and green flowered dress flapping like a flag in a brisk wind. She tramped along in silence, and when David attempted to open a conversation by showing her an interesting stone he had picked up, she replied with a "Hmph!" which seemed to end that.

When they had reached the bottom of the hill, turned onto Maple Avenue and passed Phisby's Shoe Repair Shoppe, Aunt Melba asked, "Does young Harry Barndollar still run the drugstore on the corner?"

David nodded, though he had never thought of the proprietor of Barndollar's Quality Drugs as being young. "Yup," he said. "He . . ."

Aunt Melba interrupted him sharply. "Say 'yes' instead of 'yup' if you please, young man!" and David knew he was on his way to being forgiven.

With David trailing behind, she sailed into the newly remodeled all-plate-glass entrance of Barndollar's Quality Drugs past a clerk whom she didn't know and parked herself in front of the glass and plastic cosmetics case. "Harry Barndollar," she called out, gazing up at the ceiling full of fluorescent fixtures, "what in creation have you done to this store?" Mr. Barndollar emerged from behind the Prescriptions Counter and greeted her warmly, but Aunt Melba continued to inspect and scold. "Where is the soda fountain?" she demanded.

Mr. Barndollar leaned on a case displaying false eyelashes, eye shadow, eyebrow pencil, and eyeliner and shrugged his shoulders. "Can't make money on soda fountains these days, Miss Cavendish."

"Harry!" Aunt Melba said severely, "Money is meant

to purchase pleasures. Only fools destroy pleasures for money!" and turning away curtly she swished over to the unknown clerk, selected a few small items and swept out, leaving Mr. Barndollar with the feeling that he had been a disappointment to someone very important. Stunned, David hurried after his aunt, reflecting that he agreed with her. He had liked Barndollar's Quality Drugs a lot more before it was remodeled.

She was waiting for him outside. "Where to, now?" he asked, anxious to watch her next encounter.

"Fruit store, if you please!" she replied. "I've got to get a few fresh greens into those stomachs of yours. You are all dreadfully pale!" David, suddenly feeling weak at the thought of fresh greens, aimed her toward Costa's Fruit Market, but with less enthusiasm than before.

As they crossed the corner, they heard a thin shrill voice, "Yoo hoo, Melba. Yoo hoo, Melba Cavendish!"

Aunt Melba paused and turned. Two doors down, seated at a card table in front of Murphy Motors was Mrs. Krantz. "Much too much noise!" Aunt Melba muttered, but she took David's arm and propelled him toward Mrs. Krantz. Even though they were coming directly toward her, Mrs. Krantz continued to "yoo hoo" and wave.

"Goodness, Daisy!" Aunt Melba said. "Why not call out the town band?"

"Melba, it's been an age since I've seen you!" Mrs. Krantz declared, giving Aunt Melba a plump, hard hug. "And you haven't changed one bit!"

Aunt Melba stood back and stared at the card table. "Daisy Krantz, what in creation are you doing sitting out here on the sidewalk?"

"Selling raffles!" Mrs. Krantz explained, pointing to a large sign on the card table which showed a large shiny automobile. "It's for the American Woman's United Annual Charity Fund Drive. Everyone who buys a ticket for fifty cents has a chance to win this car." She held up a book of tickets and ruffled them gaily at Aunt Melba. "We draw the winner at our Annual Supper and Social and, Melba dear, it's positively thrilling! I've even bought an entire book for myself!" She shivered with delight.

David's eye was drawn to the book of tickets which he picked up and studied. They seemed oddly familiar. Then he remembered the boxful of them stuck away in his closet. Now that he knew what they were, he could throw them away. He didn't have any car to offer as a prize.

After an endless conversation, Aunt Melba and Mrs. Krantz said good-by, promising to meet at the Police Department Picnic on Saturday. Then David and his aunt turned back toward the fruit market.

"Ridiculous!" she muttered as they crossed the street.

"I beg your pardon?" David asked, remembering his manners.

"I said ridiculous!" Aunt Melba said sharply. "Sitting out on the sidewalk clucking like an old hen. Raffle, indeed! It's nothing but gambling. You can give away anything if there's a game of chance involved. Even your grandmother's wig!"

David waited for his aunt outside of Costa's. When she finally came out, he had a few questions to ask her. "Did you really mean it when you said you can give away *anything* if you raffle it?" he asked, as they tramped back up the hill, David loaded to the eyeballs with little green bags from the fruit market.

"Absolutely!" she declared. "Of course, it helps if it's all for a good cause. Then people can assure themselves they're being quite unselfish. Why, what in creation would Daisy Krantz do with a car? When I knew her, she couldn't even ride a bicycle!"

David unloaded the bags on the kitchen table and without waiting to see what was inside, rushed off to Snooper's house.

"Hey, Snooper, what's a good cause?" he asked, after forcing Snooper away from his back fence where he had been spying on the neighbors.

"Huh?" Snooper hooted, annoyed at the interruption.

"What's a good cause?" David repeated.

"I don't get you!" Snooper's nose wrinkled.

"Like—if you were a grownup—what would you think would need fixing or changing in the world?"

"Taxes!" Snooper said promptly. "Grownups complain a lot about taxes. Like school taxes and stuff. Every time I bring home a report card, my dad waves it around and shouts about how much my 'C's' are costing him. I'm not sure exactly what he means, but I keep thinking that if taxes were lower, he wouldn't be so mad about my grades."

It made sense to David. He had heard his father say that school taxes had been skyrocketing in the past few years. "So that would be a good cause—bringing down school taxes. Right?"

Snooper nodded positively. "Right!"

"And if I collected a whole lot of money and gave it to Mr. Candless to pay for—uh—books and desks and stuff, that would make taxes lower, right?"

Snooper, anxious to get back to his spying, was no longer paying attention. "I guess so," he said with a shrug.

"It's settled then!" David turned to rush away. "Don't forget you promised to keep the kittens until Saturday!" he called over his shoulder.

Diana was standing in the front hall dressed in one of Mr. Keegan's shirts, topped by a necktie and old hat.

"What are you doing?" she asked, planting herself firmly in his path.

"Out of my way!" he ordered. "I'm busy."

"Busy doing what?"

David bit his tongue in annoyance at his stupidity. Now that she was interested, she would stick to him like a fly to flypaper. "Hey!" he said, suddenly inspired. "Did you see all the great stuff Aunt Melba brought from downtown? I know some of it's for you."

In a second Diana was gone. David dashed upstairs, collected the raffle books from his closet, and found a large piece of white cardboard and a box of crayons. Back outside, he pulled his wagon out of the garage, dragged out four cinder blocks he'd been saving, borrowed an old folding chair from the basement and loaded everything hurriedly into the wagon. He didn't want to have to explain to anyone and, amazingly, no one stopped him.

It didn't take long to get back downtown, the wagon being so heavily loaded that it practically chased him the whole way downhill.

He parked in front of Barndollar's Drugs, unloaded the cinder blocks and hoisted the wagon up on top. He opened his folding chair, sat down and began to make a sign.

"What's this now?" Mr. Barndollar had come to his plate-glass and chrome doorway.

"Hi, Mr. Barndollar," David said pleasantly. "I'm just having a raffle here. Hope you don't mind."

"Raffle, schmaffle. What's this about a raffle? Of course I mind. You can't park your load of junk in front of my store. It covers up the window display. You'll have to move!"

David was surprised. Mr. Barndollar was usually nice to kids. But today, he was mad. David guessed it was on account of what his Aunt Melba had said.

He loaded his equipment back onto the wagon and moved away from Barndollar's. He wasn't going to give up now. But where to set up shop? Passing the People's Union Bank and Trust Company, David considered a spot just at the edge of their wide granite steps, then changed his mind. He just wasn't sure about that guard inside with the gun. Cut-Rate Hardware had a display of garbage cans outside its front door, so David passed right by. Then he came to Phisby's Shoe Repair Shoppe and noticed a small sign on the door. "Closed For Vacation" it said.

"Great!" David thought and parked his wagon and unloaded. While he was making his sign, several people passed and stared at him curiously but no one stopped long enough to find out what he was doing.

When it was finished, he hooked it over the front of the wagon, spread out his books of tickets and sat back to wait. Two boys who looked like first graders walked by, stopped and backed up to stand at the edge of the sidewalk and stare. One nudged the other. "What's the sign say?"

"I'm trying to read it!" the taller of the two replied. "Hey!" he said to David, "you don't write so good!"

David stared scornfully. "You don't read so good!" he replied.

"Yeah, well okay," the boy agreed. "What's the sign say?"

"It says this is a raffle. You buy a chance for ten cents and you could win a very valuable prize!"

"What's the prize?" the small blond boy asked excitedly.

"The prize is a surprise," David told him. "Actually, there are two prizes. But they're both surprises," he finished lamely. When you came right out and said it, it sounded kind of dumb.

"Is it bubble gum?" the tall boy asked.

"No, it's a valuable surprise prize, like the sign says." David felt embarrassed. Several grownups had stopped and were listening to the conversation.

"What are you going to do with the dimes you get?" the other boy asked. "Keep them, I bet."

"I am not!" David was indignant. "This is for a *good cause*. What I'm doing this for is to bring down school taxes. Every bit of money I get gets sent to Mr. Candless, the school principal, to pay for books and all that stuff. Then people won't have to pay for them in taxes. I'm even going to send a letter saying all that."

"I'll contribute to that!" said a young man whom David recognized as the clerk from Barndollar's Quality Drugs. He reached into his pocket, fished around and came up with a dime. David took the dime and dropped it into his purple beanie which was turned upside down on the wagon. Then he handed the clerk a raffle book, showed him where to sign his name, tore off a stub with a number on it and handed it to him.

"Thank you," David said politely. "I hope you win." He did, too. The man had a kind look on his face and David was sure he'd give one of the kittens a very good home.

"When will I know if I've won?" the young man asked, smiling at David.

David shrugged. He hadn't thought about that. "In a couple of days, I guess."

The young man smiled broadly and moved away,

making room in front of the wagon for a sweet-faced woman David remembered having seen at his mother's Charity Tea.

"What a fine idea!" she cooed and, opening her purse, she began to search through it for her wallet. The two small boys crowded in close and peered curiously into the purse, which was filled to overflowing with little plastic cases of all shapes and sizes. At last she found the right one, opened it, removed a dime, signed the raffle and taking her stub, inserted it into another of the small plastic cases. Giving David a final sweet smile, she turned away.

"All right, Mr. Keegan! What's this all about?" Police Chief Ermish towered over David and his raffle booth. Chief Ermish was huge and he was wide. His trousers, unable to ride the crest of his large stomach, constantly slid beneath it and hung, long and baggy, around his ankles. His peaked cap sat far back on his head, the bill pointing upward. He was usually friendly and full of jokes but today, as he stared down at David, he wasn't laughing. "You and your friends," he nodded toward the two boys who were still hanging around, "are blocking the sidewalk. Obstructing traffic. That's a safety hazard!" He frowned down at David. "What are you doing here, anyway?"

David's voice shrunk to a squeak. "It's a raffle," he said.

"What kind of a raffle? Where's your permit?" Chief Ermish leaned forward, hands on wide hips.

"Didn't know about a permit," David's voice machinery shrank further, then shut down completely. All that came out was a tiny croak.

"What's this all about?" Chief Ermish noticed the sign and had to lean over to read it. David watched him, wondering what the penalty was for not having a permit. It couldn't be jail! Or could it?

A deep rumbling noise began down around Chief Ermish's beltline. It grew and expanded like a threatening volcano and finally, as the Chief straightened up, it erupted in a huge peal of laughter. "A tax raffle!" Chief Ermish hooted. "Help keep down school taxes! Pay for books and desks! Valuable surprise prizes!" He slapped his knee, then quickly hitched up his pants which were dipping alarmingly. "David, my boy, I predict a bright future for you! Why you might even be President!" His laughter had subsided into a series of fruity chuckles.

"No, he won't! His profession's already decided. This boy's going to be a dentist!" Dr. Bean, with his starchy white coat and huge black mustache, had come up behind the Chief.

"Hi there, Doc!" Chief Ermish turned and clapped Dr. Bean on the back. "How do you like what David has got going here?"

Dr. Bean leaned over and read the sign, then looked up at David. "You're right, Chief. He might be President. But first he's going to be a dentist. A dentist in the White House is just what this country needs."

David knew he was being teased, but as long as he stayed out of jail, he didn't care one bit.

"I want to do my part to keep down taxes!" Chief Ermish boomed. Reaching into his pocket, he pulled out a dollar and slapped it onto the wagon.

"Uh—I don't have much change," David said, his voice rejoining him again.

"Don't want any!" Chief Ermish insisted. "If a citizen can't give a buck to keep down taxes, he's a cheapskate!"

"Right you are!" Dr. Bean agreed and hurriedly dug into his pocket and pulled out a dollar.

"Hold on, Doc!" Chief Ermish held up a huge hand. "You have to wait your turn. Give me ten of those raffles, son. I'll put Mrs. Ermish's name on half of them and your Aunt Melba's on the other half. Bet you'd like to see her win one of those valuable surprise prizes, wouldn't you, son?"

"Uh—uh, sure!" David's attempt at a grin was ghastly. With a chill, he wondered what would happen if she did win.

"I've got to hand it to you, Chief. You sure are a gentleman." Dr. Bean planted his dollar on the wagon. "I'll do the same. Half the tickets for me and half for Melba Cavendish!"

David groaned inwardly but pushed a book of tickets across to both of them.

After signing the tickets and pocketing his stubs, Chief Ermish leaned forward to David. "Confidentially, just between us, could you tell me about these surprise prizes?"

"Nope!" David said firmly.

"Well, when will we know? When's the raffle?" Chief Ermish asked.

"Uh—in a couple days!"

"Wait a minute!" David saw Chief Ermish nudge Dr. Bean with his elbow. "How do I know this is on the up and up? You're not trying to pull a fast one, are you?"

"No, honest, Chief Ermish. I just—don't know when I'm going to have the raffle, that's all."

Dr. Bean's mustache spread into the shape of a soaring bird. "Seeing as you have a stake in this thing, Chief, why not hold the raffle at the Police Department Picnic on Saturday?"

"Fine idea, Doc." Chief Ermish nodded approvingly. "It sure is okay with me. How about you, David?"

"Well, okay." But David wasn't very comfortable. Somehow this thing was running away with him. He hadn't meant to make it such a big thing. All he wanted was to get rid of two valuable surprise prizes.

"It's a deal. And I'm going to see that you sell every one of those raffle tickets." Chief Ermish pushed his cap even further back on his head. "But remember, nobody pulls a fast one at the Police Department Picnic."

Chapter VIII

DAVID KEEGAN: THE WINNER

David was up early the morning of the picnic and from the moment he opened his eyes, he was worried. So many things could go wrong! He dressed, plopped the purple good-luck beanie on his head and rushed downstairs.

Aunt Melba was bustling busily about the kitchen, so absorbed in stirring, mixing and wrapping that she didn't even protest when David poured himself a huge bowl of Sugar Snappers. She was preparing a special picnic lunch for the whole family. "Good solid nourishment is what you need!" she had declared to Mrs. Keegan. "You'll enjoy it. None of those dreadful hot dog and potato salad meals for this family! Not while I'm here!"

David, who considered hot dogs and potato salad an ideal meal, doubted that he would be impressed with the menu his aunt was creating.

"Mustn't forget to check the pie," Aunt Melba muttered and she swished over to the stove and opened it. David caught a glimpse of a steaming, crusty pie.

"Looks great!" David said, thinking that pie was in many ways superior to hot dogs and potato salad. There was no reply from Aunt Melba and only a tiny growl from Fritz, who was lying in his basket in the corner staring sullenly around. Aunt Melba was deeply involved in wrapping sandwiches filled with white stuff that looked like cream cheese.

David cleared his throat. "Uh—Aunt Melba!" She glanced up sharply. "Uh—please tell Mom and Dad I'll meet them at Mohasco Park in time for the picnic. I have a few things I have to do." Aunt Melba nodded and went back to her sandwiches. David dashed back upstairs, grabbed a cigar box filled with raffle tickets and hurried out the front door toward Snooper's.

His own problems occupied so much of his mind that it had never occurred to him it might be too early to visit the McGees'. After leaning on their doorbell for a while, he stepped back in surprise as the usually immaculate Mrs. McGee answered the door. She was wearing a bathrobe the color and shape of a paper bag, and her head was covered with large metal coils that looked like powerful weapons. David was amused until he noticed that Mrs. McGee looked as though she wanted to use a weapon—on him!

"What is it, David?" she inquired shortly.

"Uh—uh, could I talk to Snooper please?"

"You can talk to anyone you want!" she muttered. "We're all up—now!" Snooper appeared beside her wearing an Indian-patterned bathrobe with fringe around the lapels, his eyes still blurry from sleep.

"Uh—hi, Snoop! I didn't mean to wake everybody but—uh, I came to get the kittens."

"Well, that's something to be thankful for!" Mrs. McGee exclaimed. "At least we were awakened for a good cause!"

David looked sharply at Mrs. McGee, wondering if she knew anything about his Good Cause Tax Raffle. Even his parents didn't know. David had a feeling they wouldn't approve, and he was not looking forward to the moment when, in their presence, the cats would be given away.

"Come on into my room," Snooper said, leading the way. "What are you going to do with them?" he wanted to know.

"I don't know," David replied vaguely, not trusting Snooper's ability to keep a secret.

"Well, we're going to the Police Department Picnic," Snooper said. "You going to be there, too?"

"I guess so," David mumbled and, taking the kittens in their box, escaped before Snooper could pry any further.

It was a long walk to the park. Although the box wasn't heavy, it was large and awkward to carry. The kittens, unhappy about being jiggled around, complained noisily. David struggled through the park gate and passed through the picnic grove, its wooden tables shaded by towering live oak. Across a short grassy area, he came to a bandstand where, once a year on July Fourth, the

Fire Department marching band stopped marching and gave a concert.

Behind the bandstand there was a small door which opened onto a dark empty space where the park grounds keeper had once kept his tools. Now it was empty and unused, and David had decided it was the best place to store the kittens and raffle tickets until they were needed. He slid the box into the space, whispered, "I'll be back soon," and closed the door.

Now that the kittens had been hidden away, it was simply a matter of waiting. David wandered about the park, doing nothing except worrying until the increasing clamor of grown-up voices and kids' yells told him that the picnic grounds were full of people.

As he crossed the grassy field toward the picnic grove, carefully avoiding several games of catch, he recognized many of his neighbors. Close to the bandstand, David saw his parents, Diana, Aunt Melba and, parked glumly on his pillow, Fritz. Their picnic table had been set with a red and white cloth and in the center stood a basket of red and white flowers. Aunt Melba was rushing about, emptying the large picnic basket and spreading the contents out on the table. There were several large bowls, dozens of wrapped sandwiches, a tall thermos and, in the center of the table, a large, plump pie.

Feeling his stomach tighten and twist with hunger, David hurried toward his family. "Boy, am I starved!"

"It's no wonder with the kind of breakfast *you* ate this morning," Aunt Melba said. "Sit down, sit down.

There's plenty here to eat and it's all nourishing. Every last bite of it!"

David had expected his parents to ask where he'd been all morning, but they said nothing, only looked at him with odd little smiles. Wondering how much they knew, he sat down and helped himself to a sandwich. As he unwrapped the waxed paper, he watched Diana teasing Fritz with a leaf. "He's going to take your arm off!" he predicted cheerfully and just then the dog did turn and snarl at Diana, who began to cry and was quickly removed by Mrs. Keegan.

David took a hearty bite of his sandwich. The filling was leafy green and sour. "What's in this sandwich?" he asked, trying to unscrew his frown.

"Watercress!" Aunt Melba replied and her eyes narrowed as she watched him study the sandwich. "Would you rather have a cottage cheese sandwich?" she asked, then pushed a large bowl across the table toward him. "Have some carrot and raisin salad!" she urged and as David shook his head politely, he noticed that neither of his parents was eating much either, but that Diana, who was nutty anyhow, was munching away happily on a cottage cheese sandwich.

"Ummmmm—yummy!" Diana enthused, and Aunt Melba beamed and helped herself to more carrot salad.

"How about lemonade?" she asked and as David nodded eagerly, she poured him a large cold cupful which he downed in two long gulps. Only when it settled burningly in his stomach did David realize that the lemonade had no sugar in it. David was unable to keep from puckering up like a prune. His aunt was watching and she was annoyed. "Sugar causes tooth decay!" she announced. "There's nothing healthier than good natural lemonade!"

Diana, who had tiptoed up behind him, leaned over and whispered in his ear, "I saw you coming from Snooper's with that big old box and I know what's in it. And I'm telling! Because Mommy said . . ."

David snapped, "There's nothing to tell. And pretty soon you'll see why." But he crossed his fingers, wishing he felt as certain as he sounded.

Several people stopped to say hello to the Keegans and Aunt Melba, and were invited to share the picnic lunch. After glancing swiftly at the table, each one hurried away. Meanwhile, David's stomach was still complaining. He eyed the pie in the center of the table.

"Uh—is that the pie you made this morning, Aunt Melba?" Aunt Melba nodded stonily and continued to eat her carrot salad.

"What kind?" David inquired softly.

Aunt Melba turned. "Fig," she replied. "But first, if you please, do some justice to my lunch!"

David, who had never tasted fig pie, felt no overwhelming urge to do so, but helping to quiet his growling stomach, he obediently turned back to his watercress sandwich.

Then, two things happened. Mrs. Krantz fluttered over to their table, pinched David's watercress-filled cheek, then plumped herself down to talk to Aunt Melba; and as David stared past her, he saw, at the edge of the picnic grove, the bright striped umbrella and wagon of Mr. Kasimir, the hot-dog man.

David reached quickly into his pocket and felt the smooth cool quarter he had put there this morning. He leaned toward his father and softly asked to be excused. Mr. Keegan, who seemed to be staring in the same direction as David had been, glanced down at David's clenched fist, and with a tiny smile, nodded. Swinging his leg over the picnic bench, David vanished into the crowd. He headed straight for the wagon where Mr. Kasimir promptly filled his order for one plump, juicy, steaming hot dog on a fresh warm roll.

From the direction of the bandstand came a loud unearthly squawk. "Testing. One. Two. Three. Testing." David, who was busily heaping his hot dog with ketchup and sauerkraut paid no attention.

"Good afternoon everyone, and welcome to Collington's fourteenth Annual Police Department Picnic." It was Chief Ermish speaking. "Since I see that most of you have finished your lunch, we will begin our regular program in which you will be entertained by many talented members of our police department. As you know, this will be followed by our annual Fire Department-Police Department softball game in which all members will participate. But first, this year we have an extra added surprise!"

David, who liked surprises, took a bite of hot dog, then edged forward to see more clearly.

Chief Ermish unfolded a piece of paper and began to read. "We have with us today a young man, alert and civic-minded who has decided to do something about the complicated state of our community finances."

David froze, the frankfurter poised in front of his mouth. Was the Chief talking about him?

"His is a new approach." The Chief squinted at the paper, then held it closer to his face. "His effort, conducted in a small way, deserves our attention and praise." The Chief looked over his paper and his eyes searched the crowd. "He organized a raffle, the proceeds of which are to go to our local schools to cover the costs of books, desks and equipment. This young citizen is deeply concerned with the high cost of maintaining our schools' superior standards while attempting to keep taxes at a reasonable level. Though his actual contribution may be small, this boy's spirit and goals are worthy of our attention and praise." The Chief looked up and this time his eyes locked on David, who felt himself edging backward, away from the Chief, his long serious speech and all of these people!

"There will be two winners in this raffle and each one will receive what the sponsor assures me is a valuable prize, although what it is I have no idea. So now, will those holders of tickets move forward please. Without further delay, I present to you the originator of Collington's first School Tax Raffle. Mr. David Keegan, come forward please!"

Heads swiveled toward him and friendly hands reached out to shove David forward. He went, unable to resist, his arms and legs numb, his head empty and weightless as a giant balloon. The half-eaten hot dog

was still in his hand and he worried about what to do with it. At the rate he was being shoved along, he'd never get it eaten by the time he reached the bandstand. Wrapping the napkin hastily around it, David stuffed the hot dog into his pocket as he was pushed the rest of the way to the bandstand.

Chief Ermish reached out to shake his hand. "Well, David, are you ready to pick the winners?"

David nodded and found that the motion made him a bit dizzy. "Yes, sir!" He was astonished to hear the croaky way his voice sounded.

"All right then, take it away, David Keegan!" The Chief waved his arm like a rodeo rider. David thought he was overdoing it a bit, but the crowd loved it. They whistled and applauded so warmly that David felt himself relaxing. Maybe this wouldn't be too bad. He stood on tiptoe aiming toward the microphone and said, "I'll—uh—excuse me folks. I have to get the stuff. I'll be right back.

There was more laughter and applause as David left the bandstand, dashed around behind it and, yanking open the door, pulled out the cigar box filled with raffle tickets and rushed back. Oddly, he sensed that something small but bouncy was following him. He glanced down. It was Fritz, now dancing about the foot of the bandstand, his tail standing straight up like a brush. He was yipping wildly and his whole fluffy body was trembling.

Suddenly Diana was there too, calling "Come here, Fritz," and reaching out for him, but the dog ignored Diana and David tried to ignore the dog.

"Pretend they're not there!" he commanded himself and reached up toward the microphone. But Fritz had found the steps to the stage. Just as David was about to speak, Fritz dashed toward him, lunged high in the air and, with the skill of a pickpocket, pulled the hot dog out of David's pocket. Giving one contented "woof" which exploded ketchup all over the stage, he settled down beside David to enjoy his meal.

The audience was convulsed. They howled, clapped, whistled, stamped and roared with laughter. David, blushing and embarrassed, considered running away but Chief Ermish, tears of laughter streaming down his plump face, moved in and, with a giant hand, clamped David around the shoulder.

"Calm down, folks!" he called, wiping away a tear. "There's plenty more fun to come!"

Irritated by all the noise, Fritz determined to search for a more peaceful spot to finish his meal. With great dignity, he lifted the hot dog and marched off the stage. Chief Ermish and the audience applauded wildly.

"And now!" Chief Ermish boomed after the applause had died down. "And now for the drawing!" David, who had been frozen with embarrassment, moved forward automatically with the cigar box, but he moved slowly and reluctantly as though he were coaxing himself along.

As he reached the microphone, he saw a field of familiar faces, all smiling. But not one person was laughing in a mean way. David felt better and smiled back. Then he extended the bowl toward Chief Ermish. "Would you pick the winner, sir?" he asked.

The Chief cocked his head with pleasure. "Ladies and gentlemen, I am honored to select the winners of Collington's first School Tax Raffle." And wrinkling his eyes shut, he plunged his fist into the box, stirred and pulled out a slip of paper. Then he reached in, stirred and pulled out another. Solemnly, he leaned toward the microphone. "The winners are"—he unfolded the first piece of paper, then the second—"Dr. George Bean and Miss Melba Cavendish! Come forward please!"

There was wild applause as Dr. Bean stood up, a broad grin reaching out toward the edge of his mustache. Aunt Melba rose, straight as a ramrod, gazing about furiously, trying to understand how she had won a raffle she knew nothing about. There was a lull in the applause as the winners made their way toward the bandstand.

"David!" Diana shrieked from the edge of the crowd. "Give Washing Machine to Dr. Bean and Dryer to Aunt Melba!" Her high, thin voice carried clearly.

"Dryer!" People turned to one another. "Washing Machine!" There were small gasps of surprise and envy from many of the crowd. "Where in the world—" Everyone was speaking excitedly now, and heads were craning furiously seeking an explanation to this amazing windfall.

David felt that grinding sense of diasaster that made him want to sink through the stage into a deep, deep hole. Of all the people in the world, his Aunt Melba, enemy of all cats, was a winner. And to make things worse, everyone thought the winners were getting a *real* washing machine and dryer.

Dr. Bean and Aunt Melba approached, Aunt Melba's eyes almost drilling holes in David. It wasn't that she was angry, David could see that. She was simply puzzled. But wait 'til she saw the prize! Would she scream, David wondered? More likely, she would scold him in front of the whole audience or else just turn and walk away without a word.

Chief Ermish reached out to help them up to the bandstand, shaking each hand, clapping each back. David stood immobile as a hunk of wood.

"Ladies and gentlemen!" Chief Ermish called into the microphone. "The winners!" He leaned over and nudged David. "How about those prizes, son?"

There was no way out. David turned, dragging his feet, his hands hanging heavy as lead and walked off the stage toward the place where the kittens were hidden. He reached down, pulled out the box and carried it back toward the crowd. Inside, the kittens were thumping furiously and the box tipped wildly back and forth. Reaching the front of the bandstand, David set the box down, removed the lid and, dipping his hand in, extracted one kitten. He stood up, handed it to Dr. Bean, muttered "Congratulations," and turned away.

"That's Washing Machine!" Diana shouted excitedly and the audience exploded with laughter. But David didn't even hear. He was past caring. Automatically, he reached in again, pulled out the remaining kitten and handed it to Aunt Melba.

"That's Dryer!" several members of the audience shouted in unison and the laughter and noise was deafening. But David ignored it. He was watching his aunt. She accepted the kitten, tucked him under her arm, inclined her head in a graceful thank-you and turned and left the bandstand. Only if you had been standing as close to her as David had, would you have seen her shiver ever so slightly as she took the kitten in her arms.

It was all over. Chief Ermish shook his hand, clapped him on the back and turned back to the microphone to introduce the Police Department Barber Shop Quartet.

David's father met him at the bottom of the steps. Putting his arm around his son, Mr. Keegan said, "I want to thank you for saving me all that tax money, son."

David was very much in a daze. "That's okay, Dad," he replied vaguely.

They walked toward the picnic table where the rest of the family was seated. Dryer was in the picnic basket, curled up for a nap. It took David a few minutes to summon the courage to speak to his aunt.

"Uh—Aunt Melba—what are you going to do with him?" David nodded toward the kitten. His Aunt stared sternly at him. "I won him, didn't I? I shall keep him, of course. What else would a person do with a valuable surprise prize?"

"But how about him?" David nodded toward Fritz who was lying on his pillow contentedly licking his chops.

"Fritz will learn to live with—um—Dryer. Eventually they may even be good friends."

David relaxed and smiled. "You can change his name if you want," he volunteered. Then he paused. "Say Aunt Melba, do you think I could have a piece of that fig pie you made? It looks really terrific." David looked up and saw Snooper pushing toward them. "And another piece for my friend, Snooper. We both love fig pie!"

Eileen Rosenbaum grew up in an old-fashioned hilltop house, complete with all the gadgetry found in David Keegan's basement. She has written TWO FOR TROUBLE partially to relive, partially to understand, and partially to improve upon her own childhood.

She attended Carnegie Institute of Technology, and worked in advertising and public relations in New York City. Mrs. Rosenbaum's stories have appeared in *Jack and Jill* and *The Instructor*.

In addition to writing, Mrs. Rosenbaum is Keeper of the Hearth in Westbury, New York, with her husband, two young sons, and no pets, since they tend to lose cats rather than find them.